Francis Young

Euclid's Elements of Geometry, Book 1

Anatiposi

Francis Young

Euclid's Elements of Geometry, Book 1

Reprint of the original.

1st Edition 2023 | ISBN: 978-3-38210-046-9

Anatiposi Verlag is an imprint of Outlook Verlagsgesellschaft mbH.

Verlag (Publisher): Outlook Verlag GmbH, Zeilweg 44, 60439 Frankfurt, Deutschland
Vertretungsberechtigt (Authorized to represent): E. Roepke, Zeilweg 44, 60439 Frankfurt, Deutschland
Druck (Print): Books on Demand GmbH, In de Tarpen 42, 22848 Norderstedt, Deutschland

EUCLID'S

ELEMENTS OF GEOMETRY,

BOOK I.,

BASED ON SIMSON'S TEXT;

WITH

EXPLANATORY REMARKS, ETC.

BY

FRANCIS YOUNG.

> The steps are guided by no lamp more clearly, through the dark mazes of Nature; by no thread more surely, through the infinite turnings of the labyrinth of Philosophy; nor, lastly, is the bottom of Truth sounded more happily by any other line.—BARROW *(on the Study of Mathematics).*

TORONTO:
JAMES CAMPBELL & SON.

INTRODUCTORY REMARKS.

1. GEOMETRY is the science which enables us to investigate the relations existing between parts of space, whether they be lines, surfaces (superficies), or solids.

2. The term Geometry is derived from two Greek words, pronounced GE (g hard), *the earth*, and METRINE, *to measure:* Geometry, therefore, in the simplest acceptation of the word, means, "*measurement of the earth.*"

3. Geometry in this form is said to have been first practised by the Egyptians, in order to restore the landmarks that were swept away and destroyed by the yearly inundation of the river Nile.

4. From this germ of practical measurement (if the account be true) Geometry grew into a theoretical science. Experimental processes gradually indicating and forming definite rules, by which we are enabled to test the truth of any proposition in Theoretical Geometry by mathematical reasoning, and construct or build up, by the use of rule and compasses, various forms and figures in practical or applied Geometry, to which Architecture, Engineering, Mapping and Surveying, and other kindred arts and sciences, are so intimately allied.

5. The first schools of Geometry are said to have been established by Thales, 600 B.C., and Pythagoras, who flourished sixty years later: the science was advanced by Plato, Eudóxus, and others.

6. It was left for Euclid to bring into a well-ordered and connected chain the first principles of Geometry that had been taught by these early geometers.

7. Some historians assign Alexandria, in Egypt, as the birthplace of Euclid; others assert that he was born at Tyre. It is certain, however, that he founded a school of mathematics at Alexandria, and flourished there circa 323—284 B.C., in the reign of Ptolemy, the son of Lagus: the time of his death is not known.

8. His writings were numerous; the most renowned of all his works is his " Elements of Geometry," in fifteen books. The fourteenth and fifteenth books are supposed to have been added by Hypsicles of Alexandria, about 170 A.D.   A monk of Bath, named Adelard, is said to have first translated the " Elements " into Latin in the reign of Henry I.: Henry Billingsley, afterwards lord-mayor of London, first rendered them into English A.D. 1570.

9. The translation from the Greek text, used in the present day, was made by Dr. Robert Simson, Professor of Mathematics in the University of Glasgow: the first edition of which was published about 1758-9. This is, however, superseded by the valuable annotated edition of the "Elements," by Mr. Potts of Trinity College, Cambridge—a standard work that is indispensable to the requirements of the advanced student.

10. All boys should learn and lay to heart Euclid's reply to Ptolemy, when he asked if there was any easier method of acquiring the science of Geometry than by the "Elements?" "THERE IS NO ROYAL ROAD TO GEOMETRY," was the philosopher's answer—and there is no short cut to a knowledge of any branch of learning: we must follow the track that has been patiently and laboriously trodden out for us by those who have gone before us, remembering that diligence, with thoughtful attention to the first steps, can alone make us proficients in any subject of study, always under the blessing of Almighty God.

11. In studying Euclid, first be sure that you thoroughly understand his meaning; do not attempt to pass on to the second definition or proposition until you have mastered the first.

12. Learn the definitions, postulates, and axioms by rote, and associate them in your mind with the numbers affixed to them as they stand in order, that you may be able to repeat any one without turning back, when reference is made to it in any proposition to substantiate the reasoning employed.

13. In going through the Propositions, do not attempt to learn *them* by rote, and never try to repeat them without following every link of reasoning on your diagram.

14. When you think you are master of a Proposition, lay aside your book and endeavour to write it from memory, constructing your diagram, as you proceed, with different letters and in a different form from that given with the text, as pointed out in Propositions 1, 2, and 3, where extra diagrams are given which correspond, one equally well with another, with the requirements of the text: this will firmly fix in your mind the method of proof or demonstration employed.

15. Lastly, remember that your faculties of reasoning and argumentative powers will be sustained and matured by a course of mathematical study: it will enable you to distinguish that which is solid and useful from that which is specious and flimsy, gold from tinsel, TRUTH from FALSEHOOD.

EUCLID'S ELEMENTS OF GEOMETRY.

BOOK I.

DEFINITIONS.

THE word DEFINITION is derived from the Latin verb DEFINIRE, *to mark out a limit or boundary* ; we may then at first consider a Definition, for the most part, as a short description of the properties belonging to certain geometrical forms and figures, giving us marks whereby we are enabled to conceive an idea of them in our minds, and to trace their shapes on any flat surface.

The Definitions of Book I. of Euclid's Elements may be divided into four Sections as follows, the third admitting of further subdivision :—

Section 1. Point, Line, and Surface ....Def. I.—VII.
    „   2. Angles ....Def. VIII.—XII.
    „   3. Figures...............................Def. XIII.—XXXIV.
            A. The Circle and its parts ...Def. XV.—XIX.
            B. Rectilineal Figures ....Def. XX.—XXXIV.
              a. Triangles ....Def. XXIV.—XXIX.
              b. Quadrilateral Figures.Def. XXX.—XXXIV
    „   4. Supplementary ....Def. XXXV.—Etc.

SECTION I. POINT, LINE, AND SURFACE. *Def.* I—VII.

I. A POINT is that which has no parts, or that which has no magnitude.

Euclid's point is therefore imaginary, shewing position only : we cannot make a point, however small, without size or magnitude ; the smallest dot we can make with a pen or pencil must have length and breadth to be visible.

II. A LINE is length without breadth.

Here a line is merely an imaginary track from one point to another, whether straight or curved :—as in the case of the point, a line drawn on paper must have length and breadth to be visible. Euclid's definitions of a point and line apply only to ideal points and lines, which can exist only in imagination.

III. The EXTREMITIES OF A LINE are points.

The points denote the position of either end of the line.

IV. A straight line is that which lies *evenly* between its *extreme* points.

A straight line, therefore, is the shortest possible distance between any two points or positions. The difference between a line and a straight line is this: let us take any two points on the surface of a table which is perfectly level, a line may be represented by a piece of wire passing from one point to the other, above, below, or through the table, bending to the right hand or to the left; but a straight line between the same points is one that may be traced with the aid of a ruler on the flat surface of the table, in a direct course, without the slightest turning to one side or the other.

V. A superficies (*or surface*) has only length and breadth.

Like Euclid's point and line, his superficies can exist in imagination only; there is nothing in nature that has length and breadth without thickness; the superficies of any thing is merely the surface or outside: Superficies, the Latin term for surface, is derived from the Latin preposition Super, *above*, and the noun Facies, a *face*.

VI. The extremities of a superficies are lines.

Lines mark or determine the extent of any surface, and clearly define its limits or boundaries.

VII. A plane superficies is that in which any two (*or more*) points being taken, the straight line (*or lines*) between them lies wholly in that superficies.

The surface of a level table or floor is the best example that we can have of a plane superficies: the word plane means even or level; hence the reason why the instrument with which the carpenter renders the surface of a rough plank even and level is called a Plane.

Bear in mind the difference between a superficies and a plane superficies; the former may be applied to the surface or outward face of any thing in nature, however uneven it may be; but the latter can only be used when we are speaking of the surface of any thing that is perfectly flat and even.

Section II. Angles. *Def.* VIII—XII.

VIII. A plane angle is the inclination of two lines to each other in a plane, which meet together, but are not in the same direction.

A plane is an even surface: we may draw two lines of any description meeting each other on the even surface of a table, slate, or black board; the corner enclosed by the lines bending towards each other at the point of meeting, is called a plane angle.

IX. A PLANE RECTILINEAL ANGLE is the inclination of two straight lines to one another, which meet together but are not in the same straight line.

The term RECTILINEAL means *formed by straight lines*, derived from the Latin adjective RECTUS, *straight*, and the noun LINEA, *a line*.

To form a correct idea of what an angle is, suppose AB and CD to be two very narrow strips of paper, fastened together by a pin thrust

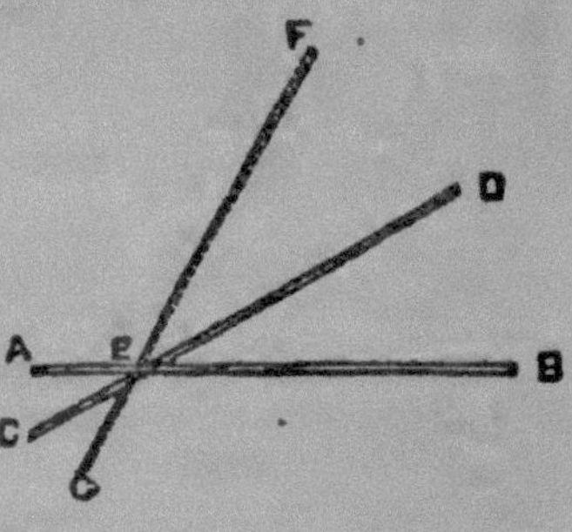

through the point E, where they cross each other; the corner BED, formed by the opening of the lines from the point E, is called an angle; the corner or angle will be smaller or greater in size as we move the end D of the strip of paper CD nearer to or farther from the end B of the strip of paper AB; thus by moving the strip CD into the position GF, we make an angle BEF, greater in size than the angle BED, formed by the previous position of the lines.

Remember that it is the EXTENT OF OPENING between the lines that is called the angle contained by the lines; the length of the lines themselves have nothing whatever to do with the size of the angle.

N.B.—When several angles are at one point B, either of them is expressed by three letters, of which the letter that is

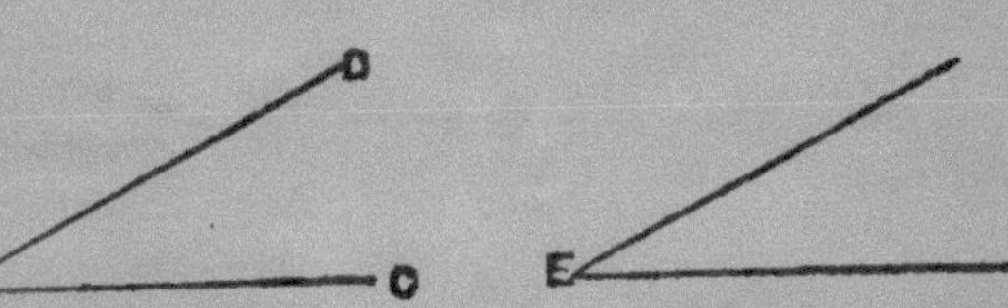

at the vertex of the angle, that is, at the point in which the straight lines that contain the angle meet one another, is put between the other two letters, and one of these two is somewhere upon one of these straight lines, and the other upon the other line. Thus the angle which is contained by the straight lines AB, CB, is termed the angle ABC or CBA; that which is contained by the angle AB, DB, is named the angle ABD or DBA; and that which is contained by DB, CB, is called the angle DBC or CBD. But if there be only one angle at a point, it may be expressed by the letter at that point as the angle at E.

X. When a straight line standing on another straight line makes the adjacent angles equal to each other, each of the angles is called a RIGHT ANGLE; and the straight line which stands on the other is called the PERPENDICULAR to it.

ADJACENT, *lying next to or neighbouring*, from the Latin preposition AD, *to or near to*, and JACERE, *to lie*, a verb. PERPENDICULAR, from the Latin noun PERPENDICULUM, *a plumb line*.

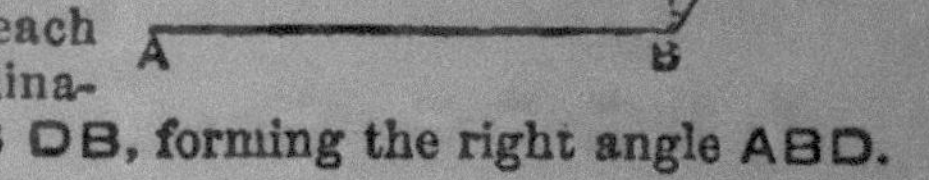

In the figure, CD is perpendicular to AB, and the angles ADC, BDC, are right angles adjacent or lying next to each other, formed by the perpendicular line CD standing on the straight line AB.

XI. An OBTUSE ANGLE is that which is *greater* than a right angle.

OBTUSE, from OBTUSUS, *blunted*, participle of the Latin verb OBTUNDERE, *to blunt*.

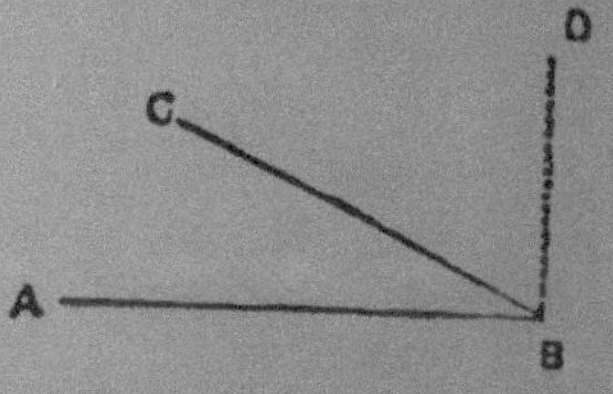

In the figure, the angle ABC is an obtuse angle; the opening formed by the inclination of the straight lines AB CB to each other, is greater than the inclination of the straight lines AB DB, forming the right angle ABD.

XII. An ACUTE ANGLE is that which is *less* than a right angle.

ACUTE, from ACUTUS, a Latin adjective, meaning *sharp* or *pointed*.

In the figure the angle ABC is an acute angle; the opening formed by the inclination of the straight lines AB CB to each other, is less than the inclination of the straight lines AB DB, forming the right angle ABD.

SECTION III. FIGURES. *Def.* XIII—XXXIV.

XIII. A TERM or BOUNDARY is the *extremity* of any thing.

TERM, from TERMA, a Greek noun, so pronounced, meaning *limit* or *extent*.

XIV. A FIGURE is that which is enclosed by one or more boundaries.

FIGURE, from FIGURA, a Latin noun, meaning *shape* or *form*. If the figure is enclosed by one or two lines, they must of necessity be curved; but if by more than two boundaries, they can then be straight lines.

A. *The Circle and its Parts.* *Def.* XV—XIX.

XX. A CIRCLE is a plane (*flat or even*) figure, contained by *one line*, which is called the CIRCUMFERENCE, and is such that all straight lines drawn from a CERTAIN POINT within the figure to the circumference are equal to one another.

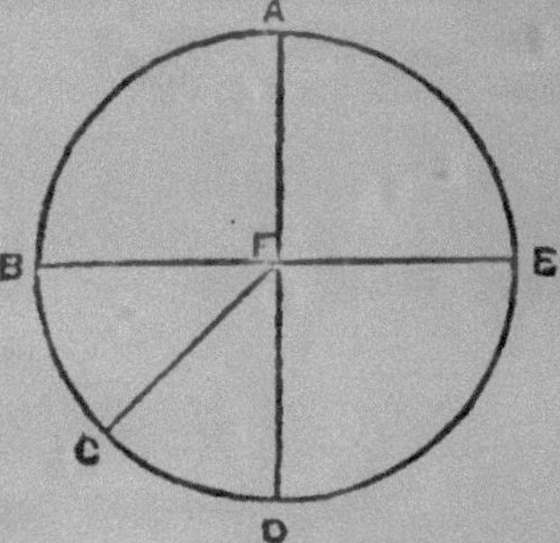

CIRCLE, from the Latin noun CIRCU-LUS, *a round figure, ring, or hoop.* CIRCUMFERENCE, from the Latin preposition CIRCUM, around, and FERENS, bearing or carrying, participle of the Latin verb FERRE, *to bear or carry.*

XVI. And this point is called the CENTRE of the circle.

CENTRE, from a Greek noun, pronounced KENTRON, meaning a *point.*

XVII. A DIAMETER of a circle is a straight line drawn through the centre, and terminated both ways by the circumference.

DIAMETER, from a Greek verb, pronounced DIAMETRINE, meaning *to measure across.*

XVIII. A SEMICIRCLE is the figure contained by a diameter, and the part of the circumference which is cut off by it.

SEMICIRCLE means half a circle, SEMI, a Latin particle, meaning *half.*

In the above figure the line ABCDE is the CIRCUMFERENCE of the circle, F is the centre; DA and BE, straight lines passing through the centre F, are diameters of the circle. The figure ABD, contained by the diameter AD, and half the circumference ABCD, is a SEMICIRCLE. The figures AED, EDB, and BAE, are also semicircles. All the straight lines FA, FB, FC, FD, FE, drawn from the *centre* F to the *circumference*, are equal to one another; they are called RADII of the circle.

A wheel is the best practical illustration that we can have of a circle and its various parts.

XIX. A SEGMENT of a circle is the figure contained by a

straight line drawn through the circle (*but not passing through the centre*), and the circumference it cuts off.

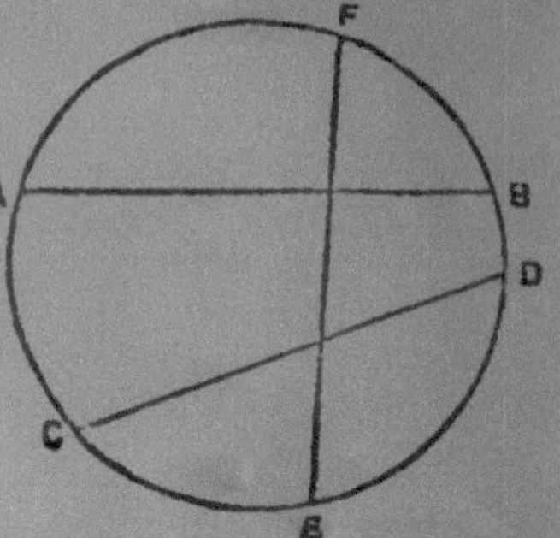

SEGMENT means *a portion cut away*, derived from the Latin noun SEGMENTUM.

In the circle ACEDBF the figures AFB, AEB, CFD, CED, EAF, EDF, are segments formed by the straight lines AB, CD, EF, and the parts of the circumference lying on either side of them.

B. *Rectilineal Figures.* *Def.* XX—XXXIV.

XX. RECTILINEAL FIGURES are those which are contained by straight lines.

XXI. TRILATERAL FIGURES or TRIANGLES, by *three* straight lines.

TRILATERAL, three-sided, from the Latin numeral adjective TRES, TRIA, three, and the noun LATUS, *a side*. TRIANGLE, a figure having *three* angles, from TRES, TRIA, THREE, and the Latin noun ANGULUS, *a corner*.

XXII. QUADRILATERAL FIGURES, by *four* straight lines.

QUADRILATERAL, *four-sided*, from Latin numeral adjective QUAT-UOR, *four*, and LATUS, *a side*.

XXIII. MULTILATERAL FIGURES or POLYGONS, by *more than four* straight lines.

MULTILATERAL, *many-sided*, from the Latin adjective MULTUS, *many*, and LATUS, *a side*. POLYGON, *a figure having many angles*, from a Greek adjective, pronounced POL-USE, *many*, and GO-NIA, *an angle*, a Greek noun so pronounced.

a. *Triangles. Def.* XXIV—XXIX.

XXIV. Of *three-sided* figures, an EQUILATERAL TRIANGLE is that which has *three equal sides* (*and three equal angles*).

EQUILATERAL, *equal-sided*, from the Latin adjective ÆQUUS, *even or equal*, and LATUS, *a side*.

XXV. An ISOSCELES (*pronounce C as K*) TRIANGLE is that which has *two sides equal*.

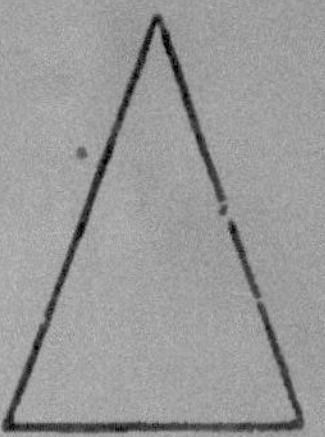

ISOSCELES, *having equal sides or legs*, from a Greek adjective, pronounced IS-OS, *equal*, and a Greek noun, pronounced SKEL-LOS, *a leg*. An *equilateral triangle* may be termed *isosceles*.

XXVI. A SCALENE TRIANGLE is that which has *three unequal sides*.

The word SCALENE is derived from a Greek adjective, pronounced SKA-LEE-NOS, *crooked or un-equal*.

XXVII. A RIGHT-ANGLED TRIANGLE is that which has *right angle* (1).

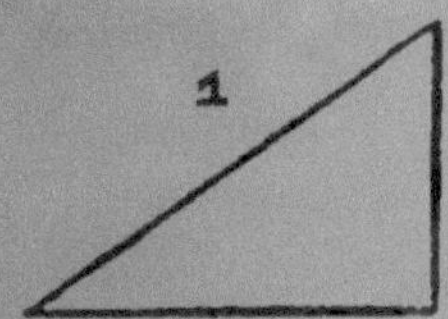

XXVIII. An OBTUSE-ANGLED TRIANGLE is that which has an *obtuse angle* (2).

XXIX. An ACUTE-ANGLED TRIANGLE is that which has *three acute angles* (3).

b *Quadrilateral Figures.* *Def.* XXX—XXXIV.

XXX. Of QUADRILATERAL or FOUR-SIDED FIGURES. A SQUARE has *all its sides equal*, and *all its angles right angles* (1).

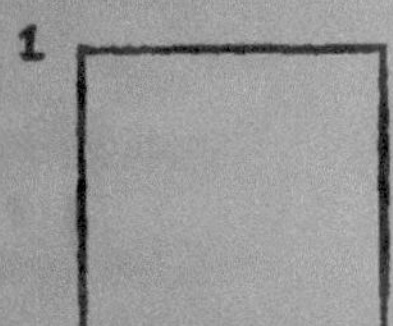

XXXI. An OBLONG is that which has *all its angles right angles*, but has *not* all its sides equal (2).

The oblong has its *opposite* sides equal to one another.

XXXII. A RHOMBUS has *all its sides* equal, but its angles are *not* right angles.

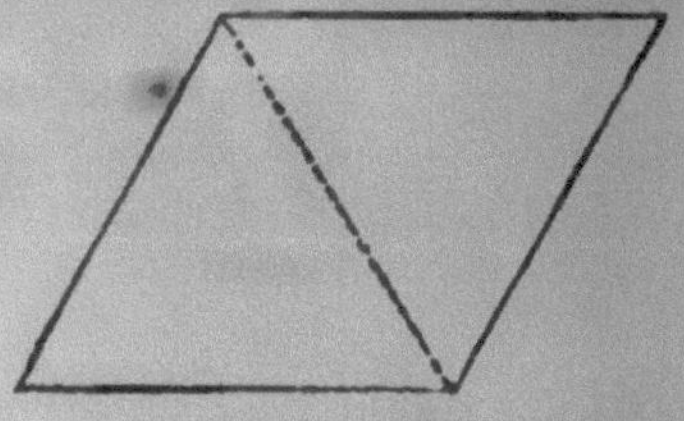

The word RHOMBUS is derived from a Greek noun, pronounced RHOMBOS; a term applied to a parallelogram with equal sides, not having its angles right angles.

The Rhombus may be formed by placing two equilateral triangles of the same size together, *base to base.*

XXXIII. A RHOMBOID has its *opposite sides equal* to each other, but all its sides are not equal, nor its angles right angles.

RHOMBOID means *having the shape or form of a rhombus*, from RHOMBOS and EIDOS, a Greek noun so pronounced, meaning *shape.*

XXXIV. All other *four-sided figures* besides these are called TRAPEZIUMS.

TRAPEZIUM, from the Greek noun TRA-PE-ZI-ON, *a small table.*

SECTION 4. SUPPLEMENTARY. *Def.* XXXV—etc.

XXXV. PARALLEL STRAIGHT LINES are such as are in the same plane, and which, being produced ever so far both ways, do not meet.

The term PARALLEL is derived from two Greek words, pronounced PARRAAL-LEE-LA, which means *by the side of each other.*

Parallel lines will run on side by side for any distance without approaching closer to each other, always preserving exactly the same space between them. The ruled lines of a sheet of music paper, and the printed lines of this book, are *parallel straight lines;* but the iron rails of a railway, which may be laid in a curved or serpentine course, are *parallel lines.* Mark the difference between LINES and STRAIGHT LINES; PARALLEL LINES and PARALLEL STRAIGHT LINES.

The term PARALLELOGRAM can be applied in common to the SQUARE, OBLONG, RHOMBUS, and RHOMBOID.

From this we infer that a PARALLELOGRAM is a *four-sided figure,* of which the *opposite sides* are *parallel,* the *opposite sides* and *angles* of the figure are also *equal* to one another.

The straight line which joins the opposite angles of a parallelogram is termed its DIAMETER.

The term PARALLELOGRAM is taken from a Greek noun, pronounced PARRALEELO-GRAMMA, which means *a parallel drawn figure.* See the derivation of the word PARALLEL above.

POSTULATES.

The term POSTULATE is derived from the Latin verb POSTULARE, *to ask or demand.* We are asked to allow that certain assertions are true, without requiring any proof of the truth of the statements made in them. On inspection, we see at once that what is demanded is possible, and that proof by a chain of mathematical reasoning is unnecessary.

Let it be granted,

I. That a STRAIGHT LINE may be drawn *from* any one point *to* any other point.

Look at definition IV. *"A straight line is that which lies evenly between its extreme points,"* it matters not where the extreme points of the straight line may be in position; therefore, wherever we may determine the position of any two points, it is possible for us to draw a straight line between them.

II. That a TERMINATED STRAIGHT LINE may be produced *to any length* in a straight line (*in the same straight course*).

We wish to extend the length of a certain straight line that we have drawn. We do this, in practice, by placing the edge of our flat ruler against the line already drawn, and tracing a continuation of the same by passing our pen or pencil along the edge of the ruler to the distance desired, whatever length that distance may be.

III. That a CIRCLE may be described *from any centre, at any distance* from that centre.

We can place one leg of our compasses on any point we choose, and trace large or small circles with the other leg, accordingly as we bring the legs of the compasses farther apart or closer together.

AXIOMS.

The word AXIOM is derived from a Greek noun, pronounced AX-I-Ō-MA, which means *a statement which CLAIMS belief by reason of its self evident truth.*

An Axiom is an assertion worthy of credit, a simple truth which is self-evident, admitting of no argument with respect to its correctness, and requiring no proof. The first seven are alike applicable to numbers, superficial extent, and solids.

I. Things which are equal to the *same* thing are equal to one another.

In numbers $3 + 2 = 5$, $4 + 1 = 5$; therefore $3 + 2 = 4 + 1$, since both compound quantities are equal to the same simple quantity.

In superficial extent, or measurement of surface, 7 square feet + 2 square feet = 1 square yard, and 5 square feet + 4 square feet = 1 square yard; therefore 7 square feet + 2 square feet = 5 square feet + 4 square feet, since both compound quantities are equa. to the same simple quantity.

In solids 20 cubic feet + 7 cubic feet = 1 cubic yard, but 15 cubic feet + 12 cubic feet = 1 cubic yard; therefore 20 cubic feet + 7 cubic feet = 15 cubic feet + 12 cubic feet, since both compound quantities are equal to the same simple quantity.

The pupil may apply a similar mode of reasoning to the next six Axioms.

II.   If *equals* be ADDED to *equals*, the WHOLES are equal.

III. If *equals* be TAKEN FROM *equals*, the REMAINDERS are equal.

IV. If *equals* be ADDED to *unequals*, the WHOLES are unequal.

V. If *equals* be TAKEN FROM *unequals*, the REMAINDERS are unequal.

VI. Things which are DOUBLE of the *same*, are equal to one another.

VII. Things which are HALVES of the *same*, are equal to one another.

VIII. Magnitudes which COINCIDE with each other, that is, *which exactly fill the same space*, are equal to one another.

If we turn a round piece of wood of such a size that it will exactly fit into a metal cylinder or tube, and then turn another piece which will also exactly fit into the same cylinder, we conclude that the pieces of wood are exactly similar in size, or, in the words of the Axiom, that the magnitudes coincide, and are equal to one another.

IX. The WHOLE is *greater* than its PART.

X. *Two straight lines* cannot *enclose* a SPACE.

Refer to note on Definition 14, to see what is the lowest number of straight lines that can enclose a space.

XI. ALL RIGHT ANGLES are *equal* to one another.

Every right angle is measured by the fourth part of the circumference of a circle, or an arc of 90 degrees.

XII.   If a straight line meets two straight lines, so as to make the two interior angles on the same side together less than two right angles, these straight lines being continually produced, shall at length meet upon that side on which are the angles which are less than two right angles.

To understand this Axiom it is necessary to become acquainted with the early propositions of Book I., that depend on the properties of parallel straight lines.

The Axioms were originally termed "*common notions*," as the first seven were applicable to the measures of numbers and solids, as well as to Geometrical measurement.

THE PROPOSITIONS.

1. Before entering on the Propositions, it is necessary to inquire what a proposition is, and into what parts it may be divided.

2. The term Proposition is derived from the Latin verb PROPONERE, *to put forward, to propose ;* a Proposition, then, is some statement put forward to us, and this statement will require solution or demonstration by mathematical reasoning, founded on the truths implied or conveyed in the Definitions, Postulates, and Axioms.

3. If the Proposition require *solution*, it is called a PROBLEM, from a Greek word pronounced PRO-BLEE-MA, meaning *something put forward or proposed ;* the Proposition, then, is a PROBLEM when it puts forward something to be done.

4. If, on the contrary, the Proposition conveys a statement or assertion requiring *demonstration*, it is called a THEOREM, from a Greek word pronounced THE-O-REE-MA, meaning *a thing to be looked at, something for contemplation.*

5. A PROBLEM *requires you to do something, and then prove that what you have done is correct.*

6. A THEOREM *states, that if certain conditions are allowed or complied with, certain results will follow, and you have to shew that these results are true.*

7. We may divide Problem and Theorem into six parts as follows; although differing slightly from the divisions adopted by Proclus, they may be more intelligible to beginners :—

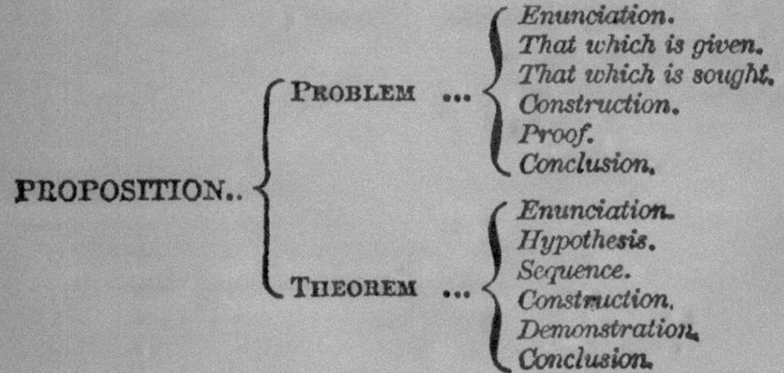

8. In the Problem, the ENUNCIATION, a term derived from the Latin verb ENUNCIARE, *to declare*, is printed at the head of the Proposition in *italics*, and declares what conditions are granted or given, and what you are required to effect on these conditions.

9. THAT WHICH IS GIVEN, asserts the conditions that are granted in particular terms, indicating the things given by letters.

10. THAT WHICH IS SOUGHT, shews what is required to be done on the conditions given.

11. The CONSTRUCTION, a term derived from the Latin verb CONSTRUERE, *to pile together, to build*, is the course adopted to build up, step by step, by the Postulates, a figure or diagram, which will satisfy in every particular that which is required to be done, or which will shew that the thing which is sought is effected.

12. The PROOF, by reasoning founded on the Definitions and Axioms (and by reference to the truths proved in preceding Propositions as we advance), shews that the conclusion to which the steps of the construction have brought us, is correct.

13. In the Theorem, the ENUNCIATION states what conditions we are allowed to assume, and the particular consequences that must follow from the truth of these assumptions

14. The HYPOTHESIS, from a Greek word pronounced HUPOTHESIS, meaning *supposition*, asserts the conditions assumed or supposed, indicating them particularly by letters.

15. The SEQUENCE, a term derived from the Latin verb SEQUI, *to follow*, points out what must follow, the conditions supposed in the hypothesis being considered correct.

16. The CONSTRUCTION, in the Theorem, consists of a slight addition to the figure indicated by the Hypothesis, to aid us in the demonstration of the truth of the Sequence.

17. The DEMONSTRATION, from the Latin verb DEMONSTRARE, *to shew or point out*, is the chain of mathematical reasoning by which we shew the assertion conveyed in the Sequence to be true.

18. The CONCLUSION, in the Problem, states that what was required to be done has been effected on the given conditions: in the Theorem, it is the enunciation repeated as a statement, of which the truth has been fully shewn.

19. In some Theorems, in order to shew that the Sequence inferred from the Hypothesis is true, we have to assume a FALSE HYPOTHESIS, and then, by arriving at an *absurd* con-

clusion, shew that the Hypothesis so assumed is false, and that the first Hypothesis must be correct. This kind of demonstration is termed INDIRECT. *Proposition* 6, *Book* I.; is the first example we meet with.

20. In the course of Book I. the following expressions will be found, which may need some explanation as to derivation, &c. :—

To APPLY *one figure to another, or a parallelogram to a straight line.* The sense of the word *apply* will be understood from the meaning of the Latin verb APPLICARE (AD-PLICARE), from which it is derived, conveying the idea of *laying* or *placing one thing closely and exactly by the side of another*, as when we fold a piece of cloth together so that the edges may coincide or touch in every part, fitting exactly to each other.

The COMPLEMENTS *of a parallelogram* are the parallelograms, which make up the whole parallelogram in conjunction with those about the diameter: the term complement is derived from the Latin verb COMPLERE, *to fill up.*

PROPOSITION 1.—PROBLEM.

To describe[1] an equilateral triangle upon a given finite straight line.

GIVEN.—Let AB be the given straight line.

SOUGHT.—It is required to describe an equilateral triangle upon it.

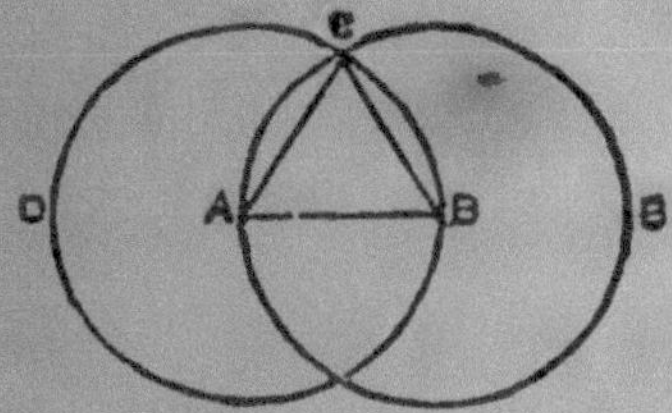
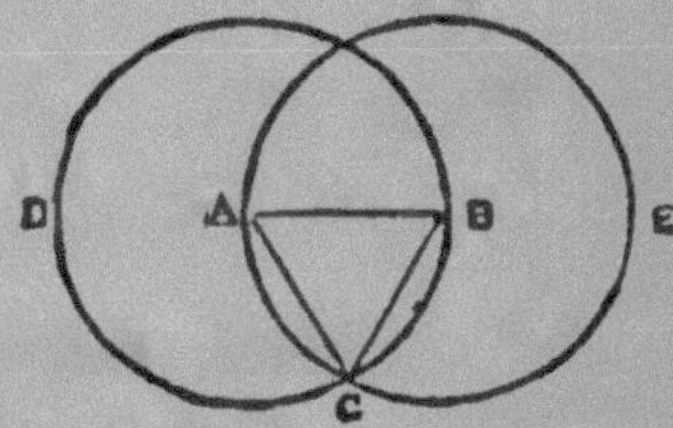

CONSTRUCTION.—1. From the centre A, at the distance AB, describe the circle BCD. (*Postulate* 3.)

2. From the centre B, at the distance BA, describe the circle ACE. (*Postulate* 3.)

3. From the point C, in which the circles cut one another, draw the straight lines CA, CB, to the points A and B. (*Postulate* 1.)

The triangle ABC shall be an equilateral triangle.

[1] *Construct* would perhaps be a better word than *describe.*

Proof.—1. Because the point A is the centre of the circle BCD, AC is equal to AB.   (*Definition* 15.)

2. Because the point B is the centre of the circle ACE, BC is equal to BA.   (*Definition* 15.)

3. Therefore AC and BC are each of them equal to AB.

4. But things which are equal to the same thing are equal to one another.   Therefore AC is equal to BC.   (*Axiom* 1.)

5. Wherefore AB, BC, and CA, are equal to one another.

Conclusion.—Therefore the triangle ABC is an equilateral triangle, and it is described on the given straight line AB.   *Which was to be done.*

PROPOSITION 2.—PROBLEM.

From a given point to draw a straight line equal to a given straight line.

Given.—Let A be the given point, and BC the given straight line.

Sought.—It is required to draw from the point A a straight line equal to BC.

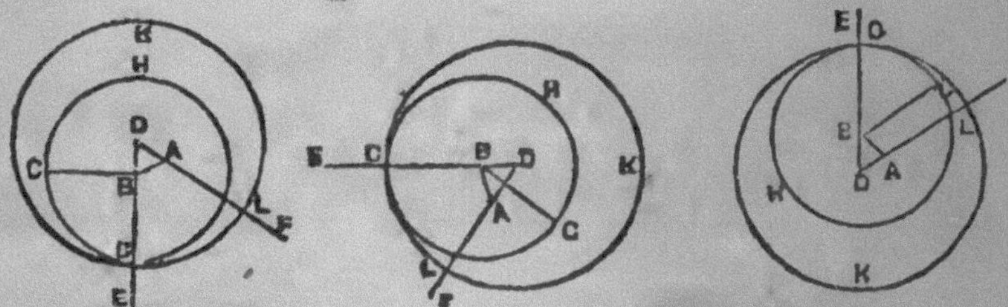

Construction—1. From the point A to B, draw the straight line AB.   (*Postulate* 1.)

2. Upon AB describe the equilateral triangle DAB.   (*Prop.* 1, *Book* I.)

3. Produce the straight lines DA, DB, to E and F.   (*Postulate* 2.)

4. From the centre B, at the distance BC, describe the circle CGH.   (*Postulate* 3.)

5. From the centre D, at the distance DG, describe the circle GKL.   (*Postulate* 3.)

AL shall be equal to BC.

Proof—1. Because the point B is the centre of the circle CGH ; BC is equal to BG.   (*Definition* 15.)

2. Because the point D is the centre of the circle GKL; DL is equal to DG.   (*Definition* 15.)

3. But DA, DB, parts of them, are equal. (*Definition* 24.—*Prop.* 1, *Book* I.)

4. Therefore the remainder AL, is equal to the remainder BG. (*Axiom* 3.)

5. But BC has been proved equal to BG. (*Proof* 1.)

6. Wherefore AL and BC are, each of them, equal to BG.

7. But things which are equal to the same thing are equal to one another, therefore the straight line AL is equal to the straight line BC. (*Axiom* 1.)

CONCLUSION.—Wherefore, from the given point A, a straight line AL has been drawn, equal to the given straight line BC. *Which was to be done.*

In constructing a figure for this Proposition with any relative positions of the given point and given straight line, it will be observed that the apex of the equilateral triangle, the point in which the given straight line and the base of the equilateral triangle meet, and the point of contact of the circles, will always be in the same straight line.

PROPOSITION 3.—PROBLEM.

From the greater of two given straight lines to cut off a part equal to the less.

GIVEN.—Let AB and C be the two given straight lines, of which AB is the greater.

SOUGHT.—It is required to cut off from AB, the greater, a part equal to C, the less.

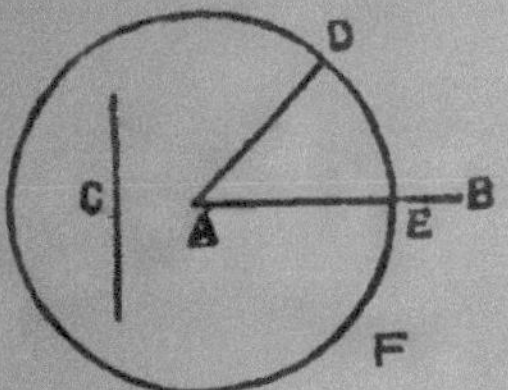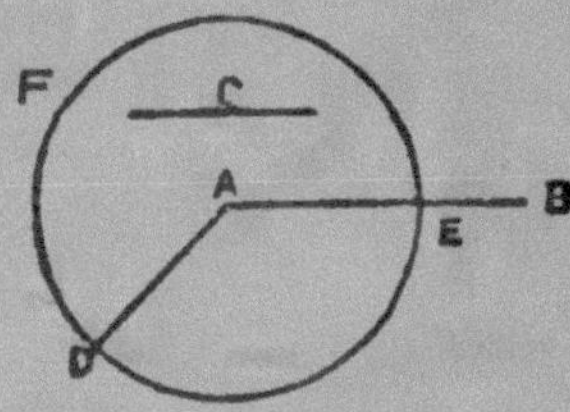

CONSTRUCTION.—1. From the point A, draw the straight line AD equal to C. (*Prop.* 2, *Book* I.)

2. From the centre A, at the distance AD, describe the circle DEF. (*Postulate* 3.)

AE, a part of AB, shall be equal to C.

PROOF.—1. Because the point A is the centre of the circle DEF, AE is equal to AD. (*Definition* 15.)

2. But the straight line C is also equal to AD. (*By Construction* 1.)

3. Whence AE and C are each of them equal to AD.

4. Wherefore the straight line AE is equal to C. (*Axiom* 1.)

CONCLUSION.—Therefore, from AB, the greater of two straight lines, a part AE has been cut off, equal to C, the less. *Which was to be done.*

PROPOSITION 4.—THEOREM.

If two triangles have two sides of the one equal to two sides of the other, each to each, and have likewise the angles contained by those sides equal to one another, they shall likewise have their bases, or third-sides, equal ; and the two triangles shall be equal, and their other angles shall be equal, each to each, viz., those to which the equal sides are opposite.

HYPOTHESIS.—Let ABC, DEF, be two triangles which have—

1. The two sides AB, AC, equal to the two sides DE, DF, each to each ;

    viz., AB equal to DE, and AC equal to DF.

2. And the angle BAC equal to the angle EDF :—then—

SEQUENCE.— 1. The base BC shall be equal to the base EF.

2. The triangle ABC, shall be equal to the triangle DEF.

3. And the other angles to which the equal sides are opposite, shall be equal, each to each.

    Viz., The angle ABC to the angle DEF, and the angle ACB to the angle DFE.

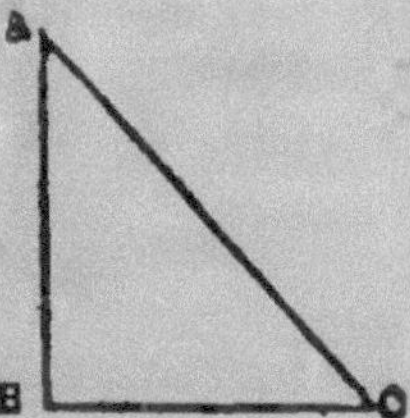 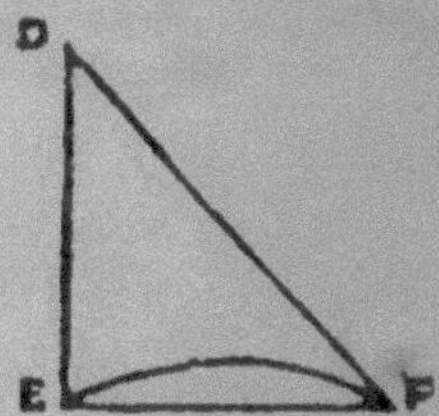

DEMONSTRATION.—1. For if the triangle ABC be applied to (*or placed upon*) the triangle DEF.

2. So that the point A may be on D, and the straight line AB on DE.

3. The point B shall coincide with the point E, because AB is equal to DE. (*Hypothesis 1.*)

4. And AB coinciding with DE, AC shall coincide with DF, because the angle BAC is equal to the angle EDF. (*Hypothesis 2.*)

5. Wherefore also the point C shall coincide with the point F, because the straight line AC is equal to DF. (*Hypothesis 1.*)

6. But the point B was proved to coincide with the point E. (*Demonstration* 3.)

7. Wherefore the base BC shall coincide with the base EF.

8. Because the point B coinciding with E, and C with F, if the base BC do not coincide with the base EF, two straight lines would enclose a space, which is impossible. (*Axiom* 10.)

9. Therefore the base BC does coincide with the base EF, and is therefore equal to it. (*Axiom* 8.)

10. Wherefore the whole triangle ABC coincides with the whole triangle DEF, and is equal to it.

11. And the other angles of the one coincide with the remaining angles of the other, and are equal to them.

Viz. : The angle ABC to the angle DEF, and the angle ACB to the angle DFE.

CONCLUSION.—Therefore, if two triangles have, &c. (*See Enunciation.*) *Which was to be shewn.*

PROPOSITION 5.—THEOREM.

The angles at the base of an isosceles triangle are equal to one another ; and, if the equal sides be produced, the angles upon the other side of the base shall be equal.

HYPOTHESIS.—1. Let ABC be an isosceles triangle, of which the side AB is equal to the side AC.

2. Let the straight lines AB, AC (*the equal sides of the triangle*), be produced to D and E.

SEQUENCE.—1. The angle ABC shall be equal to the angle ACB, (*angles at the base.*)

2. And the angle CBD shall be equal to the angle BCE, (*angles upon the other side of the base.*)

CONSTRUCTION.—1. In BD take any point F.

2. From AE, the greater, cut off AG, equal to AF, the less. (*Prop.* 3, *Book* I.)

3. Join FC, GB.

DEMONSTRATION.—1. Because AF is equal to AG. (*Construction* 2.) And AB is equal to AC. (*Hypothesis* 1.)

Therefore the two sides FA, AC, are equal to the two GA, AB, each to each.

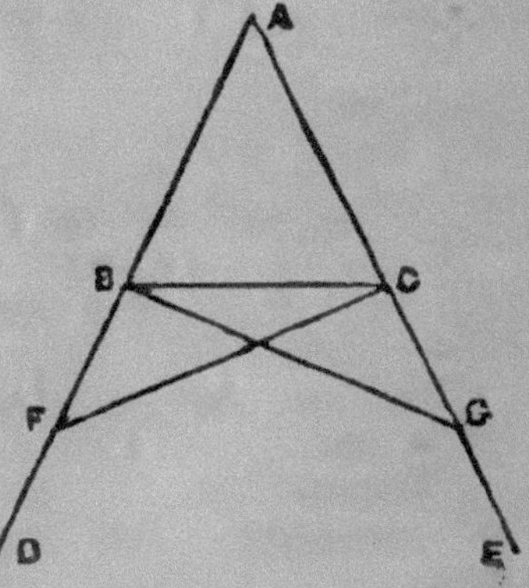

2. And they contain the angle FAG, common to the two triangles AFC, AGB.

3. Therefore the base FC is equal to the base GB. (*Prop. 4, Book* I.)

4. And the triangle AFC to the triangle AGB. (*Prop.* 4, *Book* I.)

5. And the remaining angles of the one are equal to the remaining angles of the other, each to each, to which the equal sides are opposite.

Viz. : The angle ACF equal to the angle ABG, and the angle AFC equal to the angle AGB. (*Prop.* 4, *Book* I.)

6. And, because the whole AF is equal to the whole AG, (*Construction* 2.) of which the parts AB, AC, are equal. (*Hypothesis* 1.)

The remainder BF, is equal to the remainder CG. (*Axiom* 3.)

7. And FC was proved to be equal to GB. (*Demonstration* 3.)

8. Therefore the two sides BF, FG, are equal to the two sides CG, GB, each to each.

9. And the angle BFC was proved to be equal to the angle CGB, (*for the angle AFC was proved equal to the angle AGB. Demonstration* 5.)

10. And the base BC is common to the two triangles BFC, CGB.

11. Wherefore these triangles (*BFC, CGB*) are equal. (*Prop.* 4, *Book* 1.) And their remaining angles each to each, to which the equal sides are opposite. (*Prop.* 4, *Book* I.)

12. Therefore the angle FBC is equal to the angle GCB, and the angle BCF to the angle CBG.

13. And since it has been demonstrated that the whole angle ABG is equal to the whole angle ACF. (*Demonstration* 5.)

The parts of which the angles CBG, BCF, are also equal. (*Demonstration* 12.)

14. Therefore the remaining angle ABC, is equal to the remaining angle ACB. (*Axiom* 3.)

Which are the angles at the base of the triangle ABC.

15. And it has been proved that the angle FBC is equal to the angle GCB. (*Demonstration* 12.)

Which are the angles upon the other side of the base.

CONCLUSION. Therefore, the angles at the base, &c. (*See Enunciation.*) *Which was to be shewn.*

COROLLARY. *Hence every equilateral triangle is also equiangular.*

Let ABC be an equilateral triangle, then, since the triangle is equilateral, the side AB is equal to the side AC; and, by *Proposition* 5, the angle ABC is equal to the angle ACB, being angles at the base BC of the isosceles triangle ABC (*for an equilateral triangle is also an isosceles triangle*); for the same reason the angle BCA is equal to the angle CAB, and the angle BAC to the angle ABC. The three angles of the equilateral triangle ABC are then equal to one another, and the triangle is therefore equi-angular.

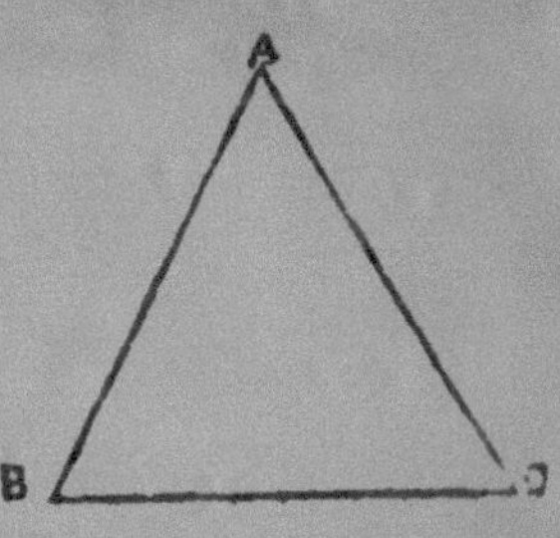

PROPOSITION 6. THEOREM.

If two angles of a triangle be equal to one another, the sides also which subtend, or are opposite to, the equal angles, shall be equal to one another.

HYPOTHESIS. Let ABC be a triangle having the angle ABC equal to the angle ACB.

SEQUENCE. The side AB shall be equal to the side AC.

If AB be not equal to AC, one of them must be greater than the other. Let AB be the greater. (FALSE HYPOTHESIS.)

CONSTRUCTION—1. From AB the greater, cut off a part DB, equal to AC the less. (*Prop.* 3, *Book* I.)

2. Join DC.

DEMONSTRATION—1. Because in the triangles DBC, ACB, DB is equal to AC, and BC common to both.

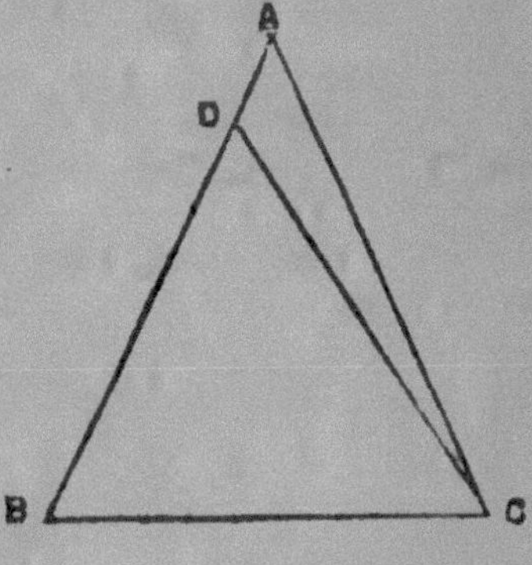

2. Therefore the two sides DB, BC, are equal to the two sides AC, CB, each to each.

3. And the angle DBC is equal to the angle ACB. (*Hypothesis.*)

4. Therefore the base DC is equal to the base AB. (*Prop.* 4, *Book* I.)

5. And the triangle DBC is equal to the triangle ABC (*Prop.* 4, *Book* I.)

The less to the greater, which is absurd.

6. Therefore AB is not unequal to AC; that is, AB is equal to AC.

CONCLUSION.—Wherefore, if two angles, &c. (*See Enunciation.*) *Which was to be shewn.*

COROLLARY.—*Hence every equi-angular triangle is also equilateral.*

This Proposition and Corollary are the converse of Proposition 5 and its Corollary, part of the Hypothesis of Proposition 5 becoming the sequence of Proposition 6, and *vice versa.* In the former the equality of the sides of the triangle is granted, and the resulting fact of the equality of the angles at the base is required to be demonstrated. In the latter, the equality of the angles at the base is allowed, and demonstration is required of the consequent reality of the equality of the sides of the triangle.

The demonstration of the above Proposition is termed negative or indirect, as the absurd conclusion to which we are led by reasoning on the second or false hypothesis, shews that the first hypothesis, and that only, can be, and must be true.

PROPOSITION 7.—THEOREM.

Upon the same base, and on the same side of it, there cannot be two triangles that have their sides, which are terminated in one extremity of the base, equal to one another, and likewise those which are terminated in the other extremity.

HYPOTHESIS—1. Let the triangles ACB, ADB, upon the same base AB, and on the same side of it, have, if possible,

2. Their sides CA, DA, terminated in the extremity A of the base, equal to one another.

3. And their sides CB, DB, terminated in the extremity B of the base, likewise equal to one another.

We have assumed the possibility of the equality of the sides, in order to demonstrate the impossibility of such a case, by arriving at an absurd conclusion, which will follow from reasoning on a false supposition.

CONSTRUCTION.—Join CD.

CASE I. First let the vertex of each triangle be without the other triangle. (*See Figure 1.*)

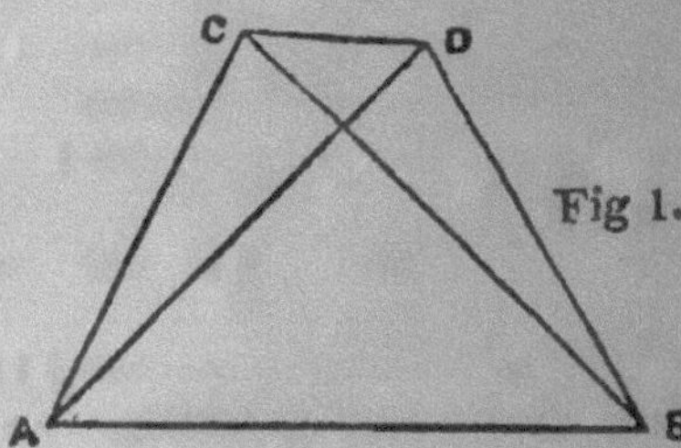

DEMONSTRATION—1. Because AC is equal to AD. (*Hypothesis 2.*)

Fig 1.

2. The triangle ADC is an isosceles triangle, and the angle ACD is therefore equal to the angle ADC. (*Prop. 5, Book I.*)

3. But the angle ACD is greater than the angle BCD. (*Axiom* 9.)

4. Therefore the angle ADC is also greater than BCD.

5. Much more, therefore, is the angle BDC (*which is greater than the angle ADC, Axiom* 9) greater than BCD.

6. Again, because BC is equal to BD. (*Hypothesis* 3.)

7. The triangle BCD is an isosceles triangle, and the angle BDC is equal to the angle BCD. (*Prop* 5, *Book* 1.)

8. But the angle BDC has been shewn to be greater than the angle BCD. (*Demonstration* 5.)

9. Therefore the angle BDC is both equal to, and greater than the same angle BCD, which is impossible.

CASE II.—Now let the vertex of one of the triangles fall within the other.—(*See Figure II.*) *The figure is constructed with the vertex D of the triangle ADB, within the other triangle ACB.*

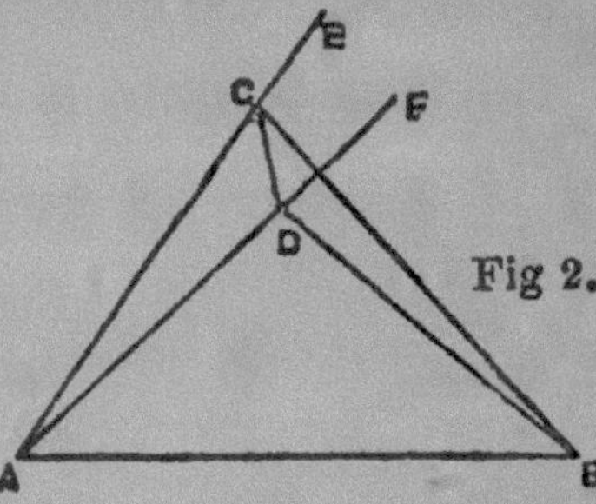

CONSTRUCTION.—Produce AC, AD, to E and F.

DEMONSTRATION—1. Because AC is equal to AD. (*Hypothesis* 2.)

Fig 2.

2. The triangle ADC is an isosceles triangle; and the angles ECD, FDC, upon the other side of its base CD, are equal to one another. (*Prop.* 5, *Book* I.)

3. But the angle ECD is greater than the angle BCD, (*Axiom* 9.)

4. Wherefore the angle FDC is likewise greater than BCD, (*for it has been proved equal to the angle ECD.*)

5. Much more then is the angle BDC (*which is greater than the angle FDC, Axiom* 9) greater than BCD.

6. Again, because BC is equal to BD. (*Hypothesis* 3.)

7. The triangle BDC is an isosceles triangle; and the angle BDC is equal to the angle BCD. (*Prop.* 5, *Book* I)

8. But the angle BDC has been shewn to be greater than the angle BCD. (*Demonstration* 5.)

9. Therefore the angle BDC is both equal to, and greater than the same angle BCD, which is impossible.

CASE III.—The case in which the vertex of one triangle is upon a side of the other needs no demonstration, as it is shewn to be impossible by *Proposition* 6.

CONCLUSION.—Therefore, upon the same base, &c. (*See Enunciation.*) *Which was to be shewn.*

PROPOSITION 8.—THEOREM.

If two triangles have two sides of the one equal to two sides of the other, each to each, and have likewise their bases equal, the angle which is contained by the two sides of the one shall be equal to the angle contained by the two sides, equal to them, of the other.

HYPOTHESIS.—Let ABC, DEF, be two triangles which have,

1. The two sides AB, AC, equal to the two sides DE, DF, each to each, viz. : AB equal to DE, and AC equal to DF.

2. And the base BC equal to the base EF.

SEQUENCE.—The angle BAC shall be equal to the angle EDF.

DEMONSTRATION—1. For if the triangle ABC be applied to DEF,

2. So that the point B may be on E, and the straight line BC on EF,

3. The point C shall coincide with the point F, because BC is equal to EF. (*Hypothesis 2.*)

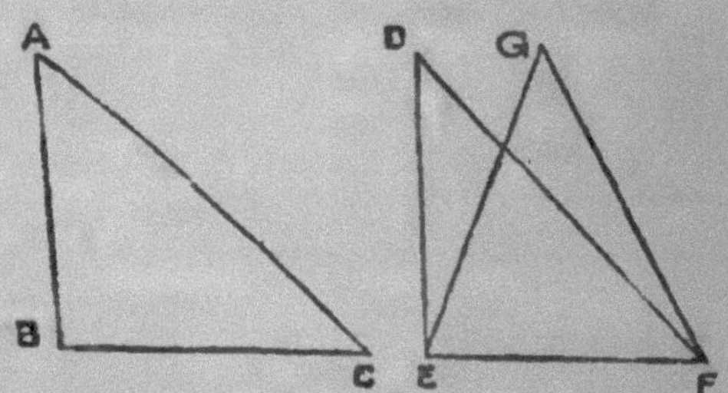

4. Therefore BC, coinciding with EF, BA and AC shall coincide with ED and DF.

5. For if the base BC coincide with the base EF,

6. But the sides BA, AC, do not coincide with the sides ED, DF, but have a different situation, as EG, GF,

7. Then upon the same base, and upon the same side of it, there can be two triangles, which have their sides terminated in one extremity of the base equal to another; and likewise their sides, which are terminated in the other extremity.

But the impossibility of this statement has been shewn in Proposition 7.

8.   Therefore, if the base BC coincide with the base EF, the sides BA, AC, must coincide with the sides ED, DE.

9. Wherefore the angle BAC must coincide with the angle EDF, and is equal to it. (*Axiom* 8.)

Conclusion.—Therefore, if two triangles, &c. (*See Enunciation.*) *Which was to be shewn.*

PROPOSITION 9.—PROBLEM.

To bisect a given rectilineal angle, that is, to divide it into two equal parts.

Given.—Let BAC be the given rectilineal angle.

Sought.—It is required to bisect it.

Construction.—1. Take any point D in AB.

2. From AC (*the greater*), cut off a part AE, equal to AD (*the less*). (*Prop.* 3, *Book* I.)

3. Join DE.

4. Upon DE, describe an equilateral triangle DEF (*on the opposite side of the base, to that on which the triangle DAE is formed.*)

5. Join AF; the straight line AF shall bisect the angle BAC.

Proof.—1. Because AD is equal to AE (*Construction* 2), and AF is common to the two triangles DAF, EAF.

2. The two sides DA, AF, are equal to the two sides EA, AF, each to each.

3. And the base DF is equal to the base EF. (*Construction* 4.)

4. Therefore, the angle DAF is equal to the angle EAF. (*Proposition* 8, *Book* I.)

Conclusion.—Wherefore the given rectilineal angle BAC is bisected by the straight line AF. *Which was to be done.*

PROPOSITION 10.—PROBLEM.

To bisect a given finite straight-line, that is, to divide it into two equal parts.

Given.—Let AB be the given straight line.

Sought.—It is required to divide it into two equal parts.

Construction.—1. On AB construct the equilateral triangle ABC. (*Prop.* 1, *Book* I.)

2. Bisect the angle ACB by the straight line CD. (*Prop.* 9, *Book* I.)

3. Let the straight line CD meet AB in the point D.

AB shall be cut into two equal parts in the point D.

PROOF 1. Because AC is equal to CB (*Construction* 1), and CD common to the two triangles, ACD, BCD.

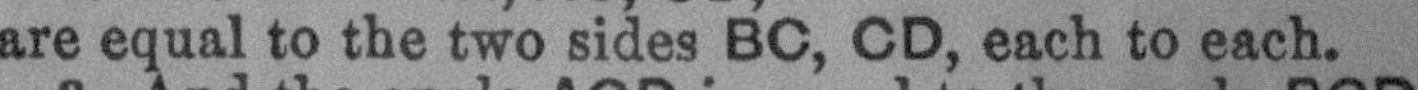

2. The two sides, AC, CD, are equal to the two sides BC, CD, each to each.

3. And the angle ACD is equal to the angle BCD. (*Construction* 2.)

4. Therefore the base AD is equal to the base DB (*Prop.* 4, *Book* I.)

CONCLUSION.—Wherefore the straight line AB is divided into two equal parts in the point D. *Which was to be done.*

PROPOSITION 11.—PROBLEM.

To draw a straight line at right angles to a given straight line from a given point in the same.

GIVEN.—Let AB be the given straight line, and C a given point in it.

SOUGHT.—It is required to draw a straight line from the point C at right angles to AB.

CONSTRUCTION.—1. Take any point D in AC.

2. Make CE equal to CD (*Prop.* 3, *Book* I.) (*producing AB, if necessary, in the same straight line from A or B, should the given point be identical with either extremity, or too close to allow us to make CE equal to CD without producing the given line.*)

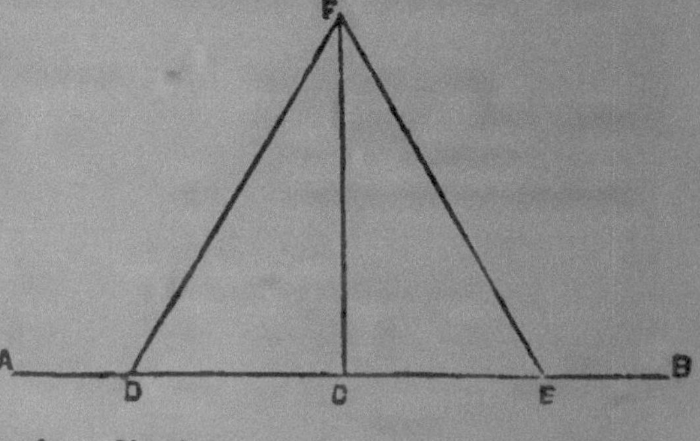

3. Upon DE describe the equilateral triangle DFE. (*Proposition* 1, *Book* I.)

4. Join FC :—the straight line FC, drawn from the given point C, shall be at right angles to the given straight line AB.

PROOF.—1. Because DC is equal to CE (*Construction* 2), and FC common to the two triangles DCF, ECF.

2. The two sides DC, CF, are equal to the two sides EC, CF, each to each.

3. And the base DF is equal to the base EF. (*Construction* 3.)

4. Therefore the angle DCF is equal to the angle ECF. And they are adjacent angles.

5. But when the adjacent angles which one straight line makes with another straight line are equal to one another, each of them is called a right angle. (*Definition* 10.)

6. Therefore each of the angles DCF, ECF, is a right angle.

CONCLUSION.—Wherefore from the given point C in the given straight line AB, a straight line FC has been drawn at right angles to AB. *Which was to be done.*

COROLLARY.—By help of this Problem, it may be demonstrated that

Two straight lines cannot have a common segment.

HYPOTHESIS.—If it be possible, let the two straight lines ABC, ABD, have the segment AB common to both of them

CONSTRUCTION.—From the point B, draw BE at right angles to AB. (*Prop.* 11, *Book* I.)

DEMONSTRATION. — 1. Because ABC is a straight line, the angle CBE is equal to the angle EBA. (*Definition* 10.)

2. But because ABD is a straight line, the angle DBE is equal to the angle EBA. (*Definition* 10.)

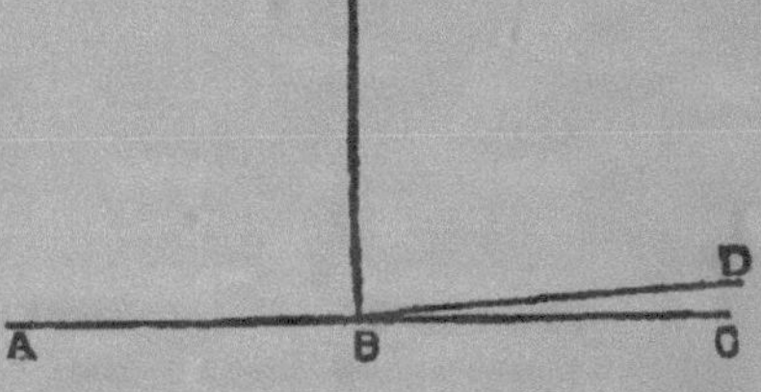

3. Wherefore the angle DBE is equal to the angle CBE. (*Axiom* 1.)

The less angle equal to the greater; which is impossible.

Therefore, two straight lines cannot have a common segment.

PROPOSITION 12.—PROBLEM.

To draw a straight line perpendicular to a given straight of unlimited length, from a given point without it.

GIVEN.—Let AB be the given straight line which may be produced to any length both ways, and let C be a point without it.

Sought.—It is required to draw from the point C, a straight line perpendicular to AB.

Construction.—1. Take any point D upon the other side of AB.

2. From the centre C, at the distance CD, describe the circle EGF. (*Postulate* 3.)

3. Let the circle E G F meet the straight line AB in the points F and G.

4. Bisect FG in H. (*Prop.* 10, *Book* I.)

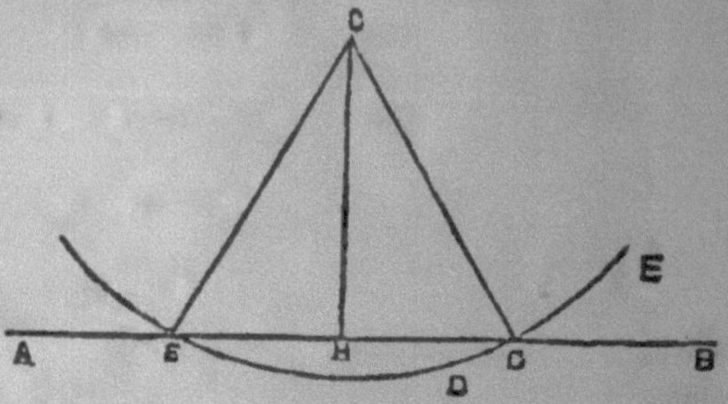

5. Join CH:—the straight line CH, drawn from the given point C, shall be perpendicular to the given straight line AB

6. Join CF, CG.

Demonstration.—1. Because FH is equal to HG, (*Construction* 4,) and HC common to the two triangles FHC GHC.

2. The two sides FH, HC, are equal to the two sides GH, HC, each to each.

3. And the base CF is equal to the base CG. (*Definition* 15.)

4. Therefore the angle CHF is equal to the angle CHG, (*Prop.* 8, *Book* I.) and they are adjacent angles.

5. But when a straight line, standing on another straight line, makes the adjacent angles equal to one another, each of them is a right angle, and the straight line which stands upon the other is called a perpendicular to it. (*Definition* 10.)

Conclusion.—Therefore, from the given point C, a perpendicular has been drawn to the given straight line AB. *Which was to be done.*

PROPOSITION 13.—THEOREM.

The angles which one straight line makes with another upon one side of it, are either two right angles, or are together equal to two right angles.

Hypothesis.—Let the straight line AB make with CD, upon one side of it, the angles CBA, ABD.

Sequence.—These angles shall either be two right angles, or shall together be equal to two right angles.

DEMONSTRATION.—1. If the angle CBA be equal to the angle ABD, each of them is a right angle. (*Definition* 10.)

2. But if the angle CBA be not equal to the angle ABD, from the point B, draw BE at right angles to CD. (*Proposition* 2, *Book* I.)

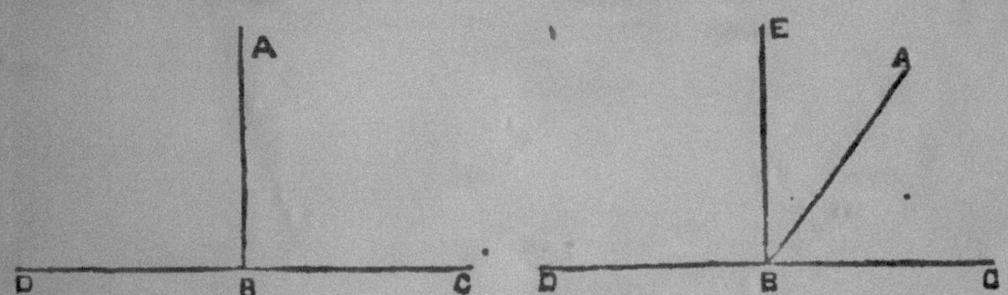

3. Therefore the angles CBE, EBD, are two right angles. (*Definition* 10.)

4. Because the angle CBE is equal to the two angles CBA, ABE, together, add the angle EBD to each of these equals.

5. Therefore the angles CBE, EBD, are equal to the three angles CBA, ABE, EBD. (*Axiom* 2.)

6. Again, because the angle DBA is equal to the two angles DBE, EBA, add the angle ABC to each of these equals.

7. Therefore the angles DBA, ABC, are equal to the three angles DBE, EBA, ABC. (*Axiom* 2.)

8. But the angles CBE, EBD, have been shewn to be equal to the same three angles. (*Demonstration* 5.)

And things which are equal to the same thing, are equal to one another.

9. Therefore the angles CBE, EBD, are equal to the angles DBA, ABC. (*Axiom* 1.)

10. But the angles CBE, EBD, are two right angles. (*Demonstration* 3.)

11. Therefore the angles DBA, ABC, are together equal to two right angles. (*Axiom* 1.)

CONCLUSION.—Wherefore the angles which one straight line, &c. (*See Enunciation.*) *Which was to be shewn.*

PROPOSITION 14.—THEOREM.

If at a point in a straight line, two other straight lines upon the opposite sides of it make the adjacent angles together equal to two right angles, these two straight lines shall be in one and the same straight line.

HYPOTHESIS.—At the point B in the straight line AB, let the two straight lines BC, BD, make opposite sides of AB, make the adjacent angles ABC, ABD, together, equal to two right angles.

SEQUENCE.—BD shall be in the same straight line with BC.

(FALSE HYPOTHESIS.)— For if BD be not in the same straight line with BC, let BE be in the same straight line with it.

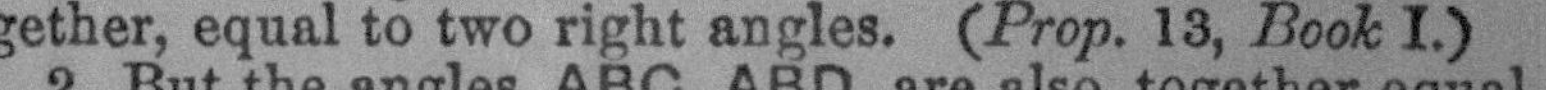

DEMONSTRATION.—1. Now, because the straight line AB makes, with the straight line CBE upon one side of it, the angles ABC, ABE, these angles are, together, equal to two right angles. (*Prop*. 13, *Book* I.)

2. But the angles ABC, ABD, are also together equal to two right angles. (*Hypothesis*.)

3. Therefore the angles ABC, ABE, are equal to the angles ABC, ABD. (*Axiom* 1.)

4. Take away the common angle ABC.

5. The remaining angle ABE, is equal to the remaining angle ABD, (*Axiom* 3,) the less angle equal to the greater, which is impossible.

6. Therefore BE is not in the same straight line with BC.

7. And, in like manner, it may be demonstrated, that no other straight line can be in the same straight line with BC, but BD.

8. Therefore BD is in the same straight line with BC.

CONCLUSION.—Wherefore, if at a point in a straight line, &c. (*See Enunciation*.) *Which was to be shewn.*

PROPOSITION 15.—THEOREM.

If two straight lines cut one another, the vertical, or opposite angles shall be equal.

HYPOTHESIS.—Let the two straight lines AB, CD, cut one another in the point E.

SEQUENCE. — The angle AEC shall be equal to its opposite angle DEB, and the angle CEB to its opposite angle AED.

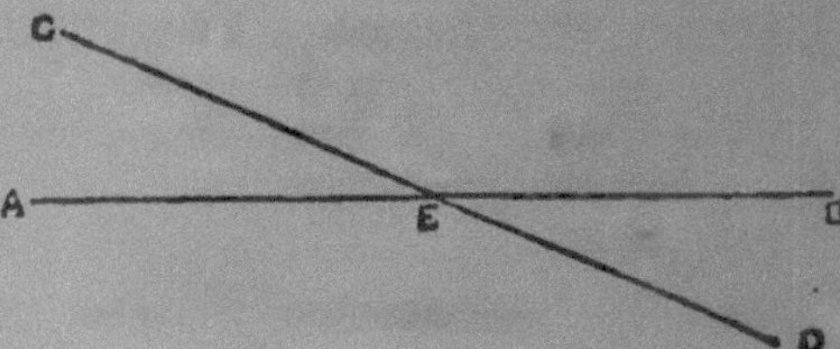

DEMONSTRATION.—1. Because the straight line AE makes, with CD, the angles CEA, AED, these angles are, together equal to two right angles. (*Prop.* 13, *Book* I.)

2. Again, because the straight line DE makes, with AB the angles AED, DEB, these angles are, together, equal to two right angles. (*Prop.* 13, *Book* I.)

3. But it has been shewn that the angles CEA, AED, are, together, equal to two right angles. (*Demonstration* 1.)

3. Wherefore the angles CEA, AED, are equal to the angles AED, DEB. (*Axiom* 1.)

4. Take away the common angle AED.

5. The remaining angle CEA, is equal to the remaining angle DEB. (*Axiom* 3.)

6. In the same manner it can be shewn that the angles CEB, AED, are equal.

CONCLUSION.—Therefore, if two straight lines, &c. (*See Enunciation.*) *Which was to be shewn.*

COROLLARY.—1. *From this it is manifest, that if two straight lines cut one another, the angles which they make at the point in which they cut, are, together, equal to four right angles.*

COROLLARY.—2. *And, consequently, that all the angles made by any number of lines meeting in one point, are, together, equal to four right angles.*

___

PROPOSITION 16.—THEOREM.

If one side of a triangle be produced, the exterior angle is greater than either of the interior opposite angles.

HYPOTHESIS.—Let ABC be a triangle, and let its side BC be produced to D.

SEQUENCE.—The exterior angle ACD shall be greater than either of the interior opposite angles CBA, BAC.

CONSTRUCTION.—1. Bisect AC in E. (*Prop.* 10, *Book* I.)

2. Join BE and produce it to F, and make EF equal to BE. (*Proposition* 3, *Book* I.)

3. Join FC.

DEMONSTRATION.— 1. Because AE is equal to EC, and BE equal to EF. (*Construction* 1, 2.)

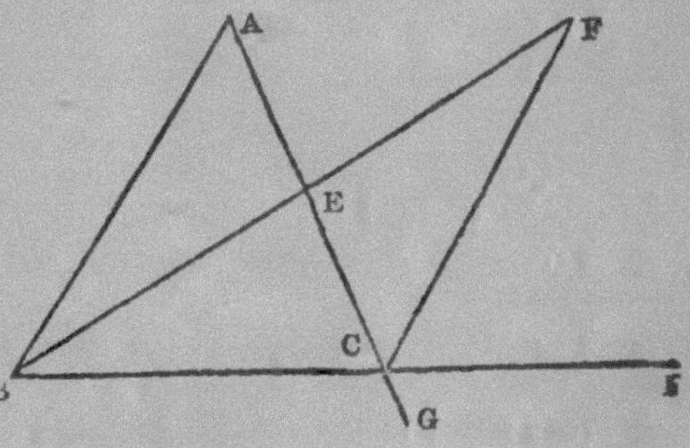

2. AE, EB, are equal to CE, EF, each to each.

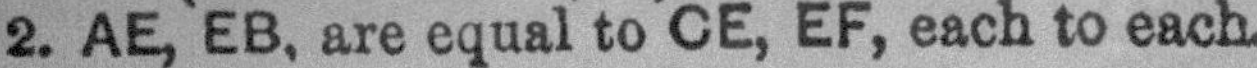

3. And the angle AEB is equal to the angle CEF, because they are opposite vertical angles. (*Prop.* 15, *Book* I.)

4. Therefore the base AB is equal to the base CF. (*Prop.* 4, *Book* I.)

5. And the triangle AEB is equal to the triangle CEF, (*Prop.* 4, *Book* I.)

6. And the remaining angles of the one, to the remaining angles of the other, each to each, to which the equal sides are opposite.

Wherefore the angle BAE is equal to the angle ECF. (*Prop.* 4, *Book* I.)

7. But the angle ECD is greater than the angle ECF. (*Axiom* 9.)

8. Therefore the angle ACD is greater than the angle BAE.

9. If the side BC be bisected, and AC be produced to G, it can be shewn in the same manner that the angle BCG, that is, the angle ACD (*since they are opposite vertical angles*) is greater than the angle ABC.

CONCLUSION.—Therefore, if one side of a triangle, &c. (*See Enunciation.*) *Which was to be shewn.*

PROPOSITION 17.—THEOREM.

Any two angles of a triangle are, together, less than two right angles.

HYPOTHESIS.—Let ABC be any triangle.

SEQUENCE.—Any two of its angles together shall be less than two right angles.

CONSTRUCTION.—Produce BC to D.

DEMONSTRATION.—1. Because ACD is the exterior angle of the triangle ABC, it is greater than the interior and opposite angle ABC. (*Prop.* 16, *Book* I.)

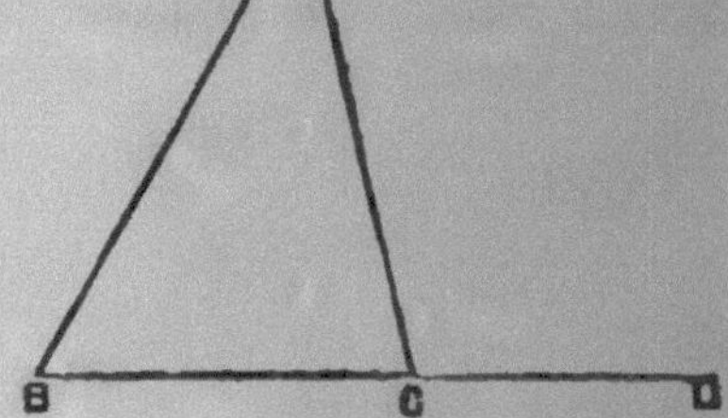

2. To each of these add the angle ACB.

3. Therefore the angles ACD, ACB, are greater than the angles ABC, ACB. (*Axiom* 4.)

4. But the angles ACD, ACB, are, together, equal to two right angles. (*Prop.* 13, *Book* I.)

5. Therefore the angles ABC, ACB, are, together, less than two right angles.

6. In like manner it can be shewn that BAC, ACB, and also CAB, ABC, are less than two right angles.

CONCLUSION.—Therefore any two angles, &c. (*See Enunciation.*) *Which was to be shewn.*

PROPOSITION 18.—THEOREM.

The greater side of every triangle is opposite to the greater angle.

HYPOTHESIS.—Let ABC be a triangle, of which the side AC is greater than the side AB.

SEQUENCE.—The angle ABC shall be greater than the angle BCA.

CONSTRUCTION.—
1. Because AC is greater than AB, make AD equal to AB. (*Prop.* 3, *Book* I.)
2. Join BD.

DEMONSTRATION.—
1. Because ADB is the exterior angle of the triangle BDC, it is greater than the interior and opposite angle BCD. (*Prop.* 16, *Book* I.)

2. But because the triangle ABD is an isosceles triangle, for the side AB is equal to the side AD. (*Construction.*)

3. The angle ADB is equal to the angle ABD. (*Prop.* 5, *Book* I.)

4. Therefore the angle ABD is greater than the angle BCD (*or ACB.*)

5. Much more, then, is the angle ABC (*which is greater than the angle ABD*) greater than the angle ACB.

CONCLUSION.—Therefore, the greater side, &c. (*See Enunciation.*) *Which was to be shewn.*

PROPOSITION 19.—THEOREM.

The greater angle of every triangle is subtended by the greater side, or has the greater side opposite to it.

HYPOTHESIS.—Let ABC be a triangle, of which the angle ABC is greater than the angle BCA.

SEQUENCE.—The side AC shall be greater than the side AB.

DEMONSTRATION.—
1. If AC be not greater than AB, it must either be equal to or less than AB.

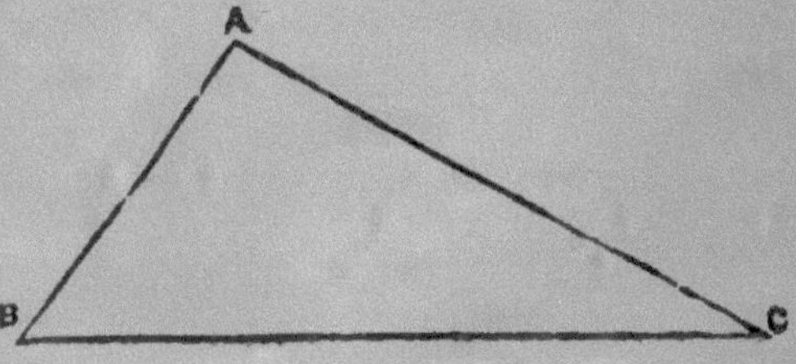

2. It is not equal, because then the angle ABC would be equal to the angle BCA.   (*Prop.* 5, *Book* I.)

3. But the angle ABC is not equal to the angle BCA. (*Hypothesis.*)

4. Therefore AC is not equal to AB.

5. Neither is AC less than AB, because then the angle ABC would be less than the angle BCA. (*Prop.* 18, *Book* I.)

6. But the angle ABC is not less than the angle BCA. (*Hypothesis.*)

7. Therefore AC is not less than AB.

8. And it has been shewn that AC is not equal to AB.

9. Therefore AC must be greater than AB.

CONCLUSION.—Wherefore the greater angle, &c.   (*See Enunciation.*)   *Which was to be shewn.*

PROPOSITION 20.—THEOREM.

Any two sides of a triangle, are together greater than the third side.

HYPOTHESIS.—Let ABC be any triangle.

SEQUENCE.—Any two sides of it together, shall be greater than the third side: viz., the sides BA, AC, greater than the side BC; and AB, BC, greater than AC; and BC, CA, greater than AB.

CONSTRUCTION.—1. Produce BA to the point D, and make AD equal to AC. (*Prop.* 3, *Book* I.)

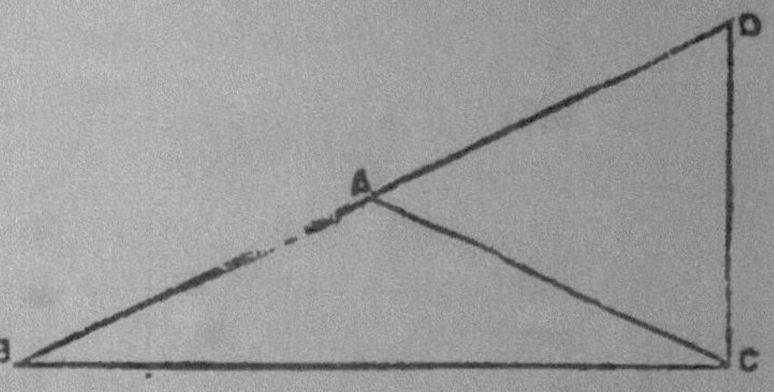

2. Join DC.

DEMONSTRATION.—1. Because DA is equal to AC, the angle ADC is equal to the angle ACD.   (*Prop.* 5, *Book* I.)

2. But the angle BCD is greater than the angle ACD. [*Axiom* 9.]

3. Therefore the angle BCD is greater than the angle ADC (*or* *BDC*.)

4. And because the angle BCD of the triangle DCB, is greater than its angle BDC, and that the greater angle is subtended by the greater side.

5. Therefore the side DB is greater than the side BC. (*Prop.* 19, *Book* I.)

6. But since AD is equal to AC.   (*Construction* 1.)

7. The straight line BD is equal to BA and AC.

8. Therefore the sides BA and AC are greater than BC, the third side.

9. In the same manner it may be demonstrated, that the sides AB BC are greater than CA, and BC CA greater than AB.

CONCLUSION.—Therefore any two sides, &c. (*See Enunciation.*) *Which was to be shewn.*

PROPOSITION 21.—THEOREM.

If from the ends of the side of a triangle there be drawn two straight lines to a point within the triangle, these shall be less than the other two sides of the triangle, but shall contain a greater angle.

HYPOTHESIS.—Let ABC be a triangle, and from the points B and C, the ends of the side BC, let the two straight lines BD, CD, be drawn to the point D within the triangle.

SEQUENCE.—1. BD DC, shall be less than the sides BA AC of the triangle BAC.

2. But BD DC shall contain an angle, BDC, greater than the angle BAC.

CONSTRUCTION.—Produce BD to E.

DEMONSTRATION.—(I.) 1. Because two sides of a triangle are greater than the third side (*Prop.* 20, *Book* I.), the two sides BA

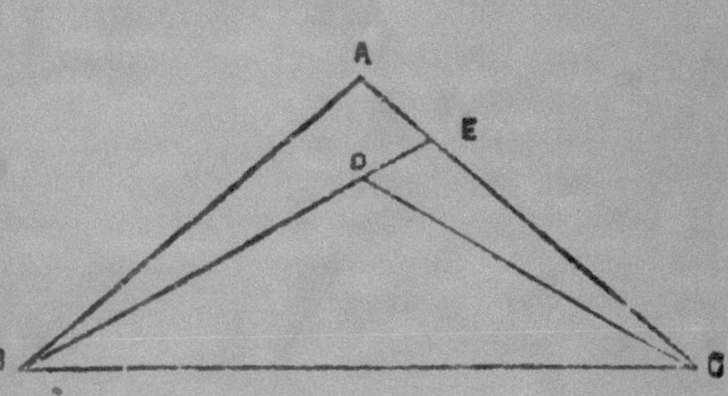

AE of the triangle BAE are greater than BE.

2. Add, to each of these, EC.

3. Therefore the sides BA, AC, are greater than BE, EC. (*Axiom* 4.)

4. Again, because the two sides CE, ED, of the triangle CED, are greater than CD. (*Prop.* 20, *Book* I.)

5. Add to each of these DB.

6. Therefore the sides CE, EB, are greater than the sides CD, DB. (*Axiom* 4.)

7. But it has been shewn that BA, AC, are greater than BE, EC. (*Demonstration* 3.)

8. Therefore much more are BA, AC, greater than BD, DC.

DEMONSTRATION.—(II.) 1. Again, because the exterior angle of a triangle is greater than the interior and opposite angle, BDC, the exterior angle of the triangle CDE is greater than CED.

2. For the same reason, CEB (*or CED*,) the exterior angle of the triangle ABE, is greater than BAC (*or BAE*).

3. And it has been demonstrated that the angle BDC is greater than the angle CEB.

4. Much more, then, is the angle BDC greater than the angle BAC.

CONCLUSION.—Therefore, if from the ends, &c. (*See Enunciation.*)   *Which was to be shewn.*

PROPOSITION 22.—PROBLEM.

To make a triangle, of which the sides shall be equal to three given straight lines, but any two whatever of these must be greater than the third.

GIVEN.—Let A, B, C, be the three given straight lines, of which any two whatever are greater than the third, viz. :—A and B greater than C, A and C greater than B, and B and C greater than A.

SOUGHT.—It is required to make a triangle, of which the sides shall be equal to A, B, and C, each to each.

CONSTRUCTION.—
1. Take a straight line, DE, terminated at the point D, but unlimited towards E.

2. Make DF equal to A, FG equal to B, and GH equal to C.   (*Prop.* 3, *Book* I.)

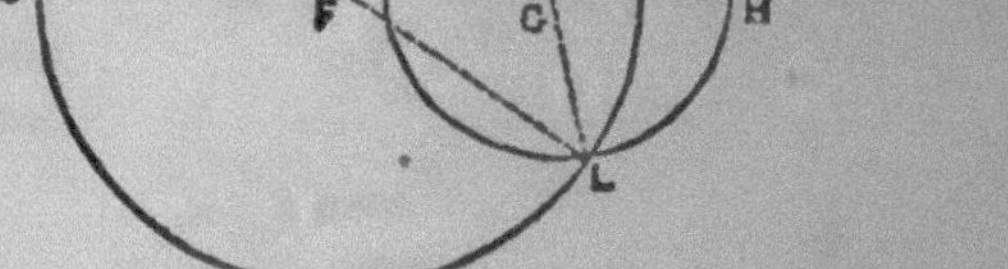

3. From the centre G, at the distance GH, describe the circle HLK.   (*Postulate* 3.)

4. From the centre F, at the distance FD, describe the circle DKL.   (*Postulate* 3.)

5. Join KF, KG, (*or LF, LG.*)

The triangle KFG (*or the triangle LFG*), shall have its sides equal to the three straight lines A, B, C.

PROOF.—1. Because the point F, is the centre of the circle DKL, FD is equal to FK.   (*Definition* 15.)

2. But FD is equal to the straight line A.   (*Construction* 2.)

3. Therefore FK is equal to the straight line A.   (*Axiom* 1.)

4. Again, because the point **G** is the centre of the circle **HLK**, **GH** is equal to **GK**. (*Definition* 15.)

5. But **GH** is equal to the straight line **C**. (*Construction* 2.)

6. Therefore **GK** is equal to the straight line **C**. (*Axiom* 1.)

7. And **FG** is equal to the straight line **B**. (*Construction* 2.)

8. Therefore the three straight lines **KF**, **FG**, **GK**, are equal to the three straight lines **A**, **B**, **C**, each to each.

CONCLUSION.—Therefore the triangle **KFG** has its three sides, **KF**, **FG**, **GK**, equal to the three given straight lines, **A**, **B**, **C**. *Which was to be done.*

A similar mode of proof will shew that the triangle LFG also has its three sides, LF, FG, GL, equal to the three given straight lines A, B, C.

PROPOSITION 23.—PROBLEM.

At a given point in a given straight line, to make a rectilineal angle equal to a given rectilineal angle.

GIVEN—1. Let **AB** be the given straight line, and **A** the given point in it.

2. And let **DCE** be the given rectilineal angle.

SOUGHT.—It is required to make an angle at the given point **A**, in the straight line **AB**, that shall be equal to the given rectilineal angle, **DCE**.

CONSTRUCTION.—1. In **CD**, **CE**, (*the sides which contain the given rectilineal angle DCE*), take any points, **D**, **E**.

2. Join **DE**.

3. On **AB**, construct a triangle **AFG**, the sides of which

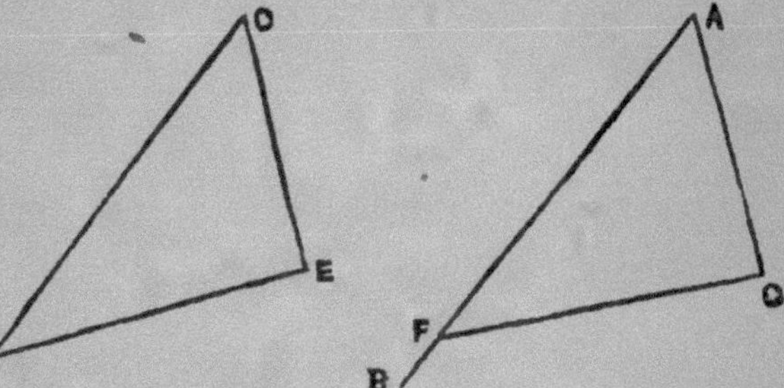

shall be equal to the three straight lines **CD**, **DE**, **EC**. (*Prop.* 22, *Book* I.)

VIZ.—**AF** equal to **CD**, **FG** equal to **DE**, and **EC** equal to **GA**.

The angle **FAG** shall be equal to the angle **DCE**.

PROOF.—1. Because **DC**, **CE** are equal to **FA**, **AG**, each to each, and the base DE equal to the base FG. (*Construction* 3.)

2. The angle DCE is equal to the angle FAG. (*Prop.* 8, *Book* I.)

CONCLUSION.—Therefore at the given point A, in the given straight line AB, the angle FAG is made equal to the given rectilineal angle DCE. *Which was to be done.*

PROPOSITION 24.—THEOREM.

If two triangles have two sides of the one equal to two sides of the other, each to each, but the angle contained by the two sides of one of them, greater than the angle contained by the two sides equal to them of the other, the base of that which has the greater angle shall be greater than the base of the other.

HYPOTHESIS.—Let ABC, DEF, be two triangles, which have,

1. The two sides AB, AC, equal to the two DE, DF, each to each; viz., AB equal to DE, and AC to DF.

2. But the angle BAC greater than the angle EDF.

SEQUENCE.—The base BC shall be greater than the base EF.

CONSTRUCTION.—
1. Let the side DF of the triangle DEF, be greater than its side DE.

2. Then at the point D, in the straight line ED, make the angle EDG equal to the angle BAC. (*Prop.* 23, *Book* I.)

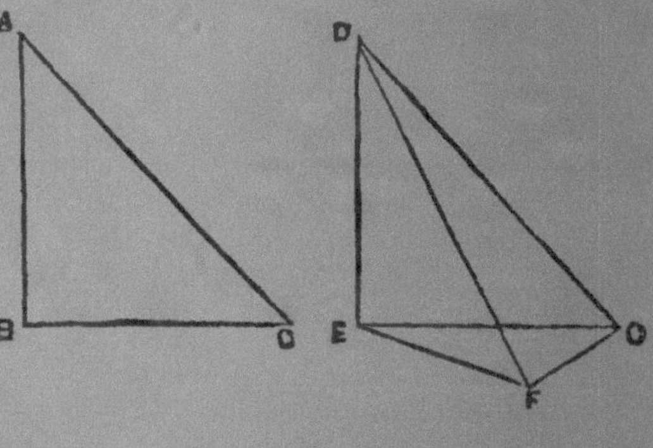

3. Make DG equal to DF or AC. (*Prop.* 3, *Book* I.)
4. Join EG GF.

DEMONSTRATION.—1. Because AB is equal to DE, (*Hypothesis* 1,) and AC to DG, (*Construction* 3,) the two sides BA, AC, are equal to the two ED, DG, each to each.

2. And the angle BAC is equal to the angle EDG. (*Construction* 2.)

3. Therefore the base BC is equal to the base EG. (*Prop.* 4, *Book* I.)

4. And because DG is equal to DF, (*Construction* 3,)

(the triangle DFG is an isosceles triangle, and) the angle DFG is equal to the angle DGF. *(Prop. 5, Book I.)*

5. But the angle DGF is greater than the angle EGF. *(Axiom 9.)*

6. Therefore the angle DFG is greater than the angle EGF.

7. Much more then is the angle EFG *(which is greater than DFG, Axiom 9,)* greater than the angle EGF.

8. And because the angle EFG of the triangle EFG, is greater than its angle EGF, and that the greater angle is subtended by the greater side.

9. Therefore the side EG, is greater than the side EF. *(Prop. 19, Book I.)*

10. But EG was proved to be equal to BC.

11. Therefore BC is greater than EF.

CONCLUSION.—Therefore if two triangles, &c. *(See Enunciation.)* *Which was to be done.*

PROPOSITION 25.—THEOREM.

If two triangles have two sides of the one equal to two sides of the other, each to each, but the base of the one greater than the base of the other, the angle contained by the sides of that which has the greater base, shall be greater than the angle contained by the sides equal to them of the other.

HYPOTHESIS.—Let ABC, DEF, be two triangles, which have—

1. The two sides AB, AC, equal to the two sides DE, DF, each to each; viz., AB equal to DE, and AC equal to DF.

2. But the base BC, greater than the base EF.

SEQUENCE.—The angle BAC shall be greater than the angle EDF.

DEMONSTRATION.—1. For if it be not greater, it must be either equal to it or less than it.

2. But the angle BAC is not equal to the angle EDF, because then the base BC would be equal to the base EF. *(Prop. 4, Book I.)*

3. But the base BC is not equal to the base EF *(Hypothesis 2.)*

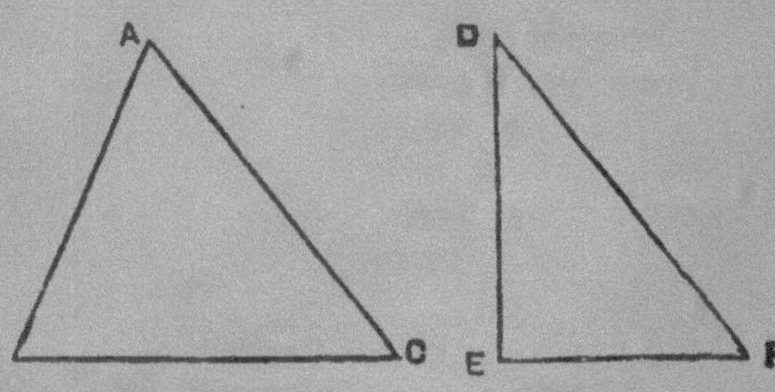

4. Therefore the angle BAC is not equal to the angle EDF.

5. And the angle BAC is not less than the angle EDF, because then the base BC would be less than the base EF. (*Proposition* 24, *Book* I.)

6. But the base BC is not less than the base EF. (*Hypothesis* 2.)

7. Therefore the angle BAC is not less than the angle EDF.

8. And it was shewn that the angle BAC is not equal to the angle EDF. (*Demonstration* 4.)

9. Therefore the angle BAC must be greater than the angle EDF.

Conclusion.—Therefore, if two triangles, &c. (*See Enunciation.*) *Which was to be shewn.*

PROPOSITION 26.—THEOREM.

If two triangles have two angles of the one equal to two angles of the other, each to each, and one side equal to one side; viz., either the sides adjacent to the equal angles (1), or the sides opposite to the equal angles (2), in each, then shall the other sides be equal, each to each, and also the third angle of the one to the third angle of the other.

Hypothesis.—Let ABC, DEF, be two triangles, which have—

1. The angles ABC, BCA, equal to the angles DEF, EFD, each to each; viz., ABC to DEF, and BCA to EFD.

2. Also one side equal to one side.

Case 1.—First, let those sides be equal which are adjacent to the angles that are equal in the two triangles; viz., BC equal to EF.

Sequence.—1. The other sides shall be equal each to each; viz., AB to DE, and AC to DF.

2. And the third angle BAC, shall be equal to the third angle EDF.

Hypothesis.—(II.) For if AB be not equal to DE, one of them must be greater than the other: let AB be the greater of the two.

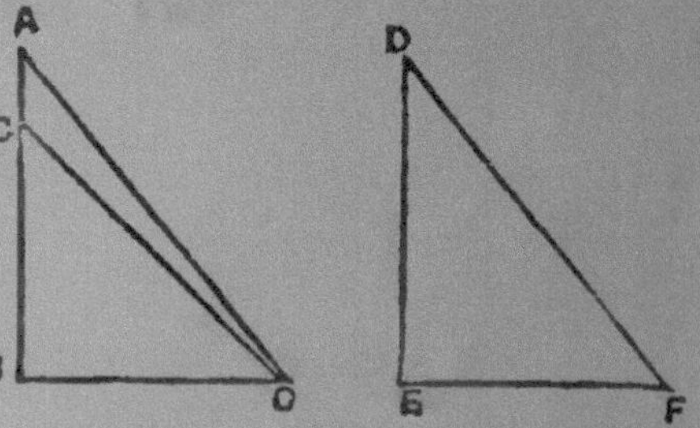

Construction.—1. Make BG equal to DE (*Proposition* 3, *Book* I.)

2. Join GC.

DEMONSTRATION.—1. Because BG is equal to DE, (*Construction* 1,) and BC equal to EF, (*Hypothesis* 2,) the two sides GB, BC, are equal to the two sides DE, EF, each to each.

2. And the angle GBC is equal to the angle DEF. (*Hypothesis* 1.)

3 Therefore the base GC is equal to the base DF. (*Proposition* 4, *Book* I.)

4. And the triangle GBC, to the triangle DEF. (*Proposition* 4, *Book* I.)

5. And the other angles to the other angles, each to each, to which the equal sides are opposite.

6. Therefore the angle GCB is equal to the angle DFE. (*Proposition* 4, *Book* I.)

7. But the angle DFE is equal to the angle BCA. (*Hypothesis* 1.)

8. Therefore the angle GCB is equal to the angle BCA. (*Axiom* 1,) the less equal to the greater, which is impossible.

9. Therefore AB is not unequal to DE; that is, AB is equal to DE; and BC is equal to EF. (*Hypothesis* 2.)

10. Therefore the two, AB, BC, are equal to the two, DE EF, each to each.

11. And the angle ABC is equal to the angle DEF (*Hypothesis* 1.)

12. Therefore the base AC is equal to the base DF. (*Proposition* 4, *Book* I.)

13. And the third angle BAC, to the third angle EDF.

CASE II.—(HYPOTHESIS.) Next, let the sides which are opposite to equal angles in each triangle, be equal to one another; viz., AB equal to DE.

SEQUENCE.—1. Likewise in this case the other sides shall be equal; viz.,—AC to DF, and BC to EF.

2. And also the third angle BAC to the third angle EDF.

HYPOTHESIS.—(II.) For if BC be not equal to EF, one of them must be greater than the other: let BC be the greater of the two.

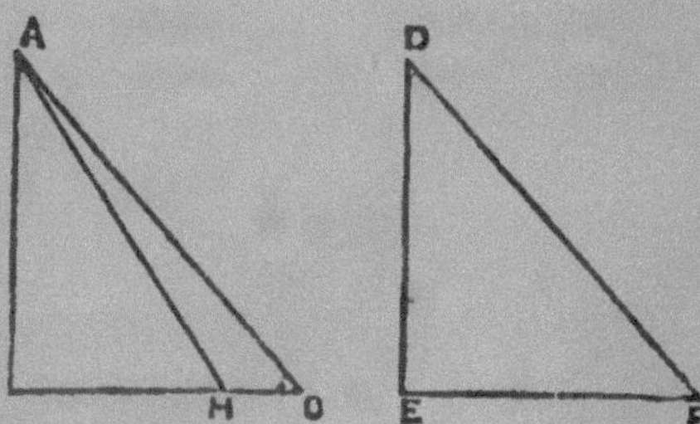

CONSTRUCTION.—1. Make BH equal to EF. (*Proposition* 3, *Book* I.)

2. Join AH.

DEMONSTRATION.—1. Because BH is equal to EF, (*Construction* 1), and AB equal to DE, (*Hypothesis*), the two sides AB BH, are equal to the two sides DE EF, each to each.

2, And the angle ABH is equal to the angle DEF. (*Hypothesis.*)

3. Therefore the base AH is equal to the base DF. (*Proposition* 4, *Book* I.)

4. And the triangle ABH to the triangle DEF. (*Proposition* 4, *Book* I.)

5. And the other angles to the other angles, each to each, to which the equal sides are opposite.

6. Therefore the angle BHA is equal to the angle EFD. (*Proposition* 4, *Book* I.)

7. But the angle EFD is equal to the angle BCA. (*Hypothesis* 1.)

8. Therefore the angle BHA is also equal to the angle BCA. (*Axiom* 1.)

9. That is, the exterior angle BHA of the triangle AHC, is equal to its interior and opposite angle BCA, which is impossible. (*Proposition* 16, *Book* I.)

10. Therefore BC is not unequal to EF; that is, BC is equal to EF; and AB is equal to DE. (*Hypothesis.*)

11. Therefore the two, AB, BC, are equal to the two, DE, EF, each to each.

12. And the angle ABC is equal to the angle DEF. (*Hypothesis* 1.)

13. Wherefore the base AC is equal to the base DF. (*Proposition* 4, *Book* I.)

14. And the third angle BAC is equal to the third angle EDF.

CONCLUSION.— Therefore if two triangles, &c. (*See Enunciation.*) *Which was to be shewn.*

PROPOSITION 27.—THEOREM.

If a straight line falling upon two other straight lines make the alternate angles equal to one another, these two straight lines shall be parallel.

HYPOTHESIS.—Let the straight line EF, which falls upon the two straight lines AB, CD, make the alternate angles AEF, EFD, equal to one another.

SEQUENCE.—AB shall be parallel to CD.

HYPOTHESIS.—(II.) For, if they be not parallel, AB and CD being produced, will meet either towards B, D, or towards A, C; let them be produced, and meet towards B and D in the point G.

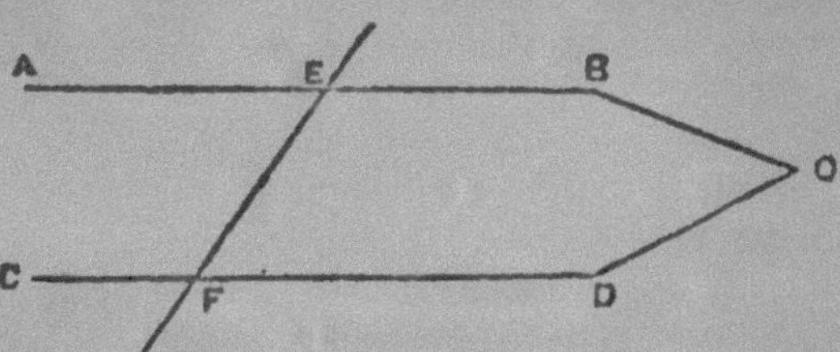

DEMONSTRATION.

—1. Now, by *Hypothesis* II., GEF is a triangle.

2. And its exterior angle, AEF, is greater than the interior and opposite angle, EFG (*Prop.* 16, *Book* I.)

3. But the angle, AEF, is also equal to EFG (*Hypothesis*), which is impossible.

4. Therefore AB and CD being produced, do not meet towards B, D.

5. In like manner it may be shewn that they do not meet towards A, C.

6. But those straight lines which meet neither way, though produced ever so far, are parallel to one another. (*Def.* 35.)

7. Therefore AB is parallel to CD.

CONCLUSION.—Wherefore if a straight line, &c. (*See Enunciation.*) *Which was to be shewn.*

PROPOSITION 28.—THEOREM.

If a straight line falling upon two other straight lines make the exterior angle equal to the interior and opposite upon the same side of the line, or make the interior angles upon the same side together equal to two right angles, the two straight lines shall be parallel to one another.

HYPOTHESIS.—Let the straight line EF, which falls upon the two straight lines, AB, CD, make,

1. The exterior angle, EGB, equal to the interior and opposite angle, GHD, upon the same side;

2. Or make the interior angles on the same side, the angles BGH, GHD, together equal to two right angles.

SEQUENCE.—AB shall be parallel to CD.

DEMONSTRATION.—(I.) 1. Because the angle EGB is equal to the angle GHD, (*Hypothesis* 1.)

2. And the angle EGB is equal to the angle AGH, (*Prop.* 15, *Book* I.)

3. Therefore the angle AGH is equal to the angle GHD (*Axiom* 1), and these angles are alternate angles.

4. Therefore AB is parallel to CD. (*Prop.* 27, *Book* I.)

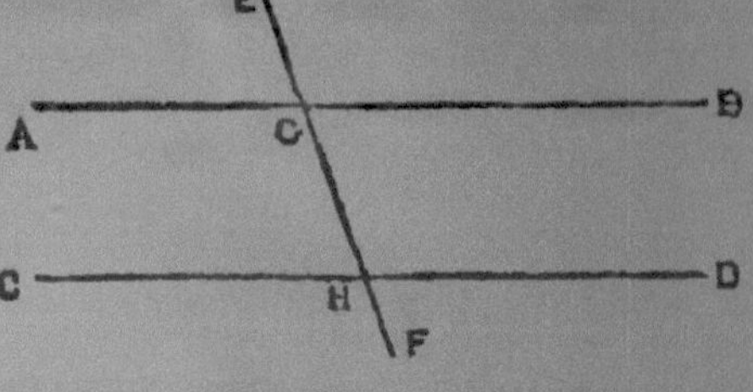

(II.) 1. Again, because the angles BGH, GHD, are equal to two right angles, (*Hypothesis* 2.)

2. And that the angles AGH, BGH, are also equal to two right angles, (*Proposition* 13, *Book* I.)

3. Therefore the angles AGH, BGH, are equal to the angles BGH, GHD. (*Axiom* 1.)

4. Take away the common angle, BGH.

5. Therefore the remaining angle, AGH, is equal to the remaining angle GHD (*Axiom* 1.), and these angles are alternate angles.

6. Therefore AB is parallel to CD. (*Prop.* 27, *Book* I.)

CONCLUSION.—Wherefore, if a straight line, &c. (*See Enunciation.*) *Which was to be shewn.*

PROPOSITION 29.—THEOREM.

If a straight line fall upon two parallel straight lines, it makes the alternate angles equal to one another, and the exterior angle equal to the interior and opposite upon the same side, and, likewise, the two interior angles upon the same side, together equal to two right angles.

HYPOTHESIS.—Let the straight line EF fall upon the parallel straight lines AB, CD.

SEQUENCE.—1. The alternate angles, AGH, GHD, shall be equal to one another.

2. The exterior angle, EGB, shall be equal to GHD, the interior and opposite angle upon the same side.

3. And the two interior angles, BGH, GHD, upon the same side, shall be together equal to two right angles.

HYPOTHESIS.—(II.) For if AGH be not equal to GHD, one of them must be greater than the other; let AGH be the greater.

DEMONSTRATION.—1. Now, because the angle **AGH** is greater than the angle **GHD**, add to each of these the angle **BGH**.

2. Therefore the angles **AGH, BGH**, are greater than the angles **BGH, GHD**. (*Axiom* 4.)

3. But the angles **AGH, BGH**, are equal to two right angles. (*Prop.* 13, *Book* I.)

4. Therefore the angles **BGH, GHD**, are less than two right angles.

5. But those straight lines which, with another straight line falling upon them, make the interior angles on the same side together less than two right angles, will meet together if they be produced far enough. (*Axiom* 12.)

6. Therefore the straight lines **AB, CD**, will meet if produced far enough.

7. But they cannot meet, because they are parallel straight lines. (*Hypothesis.*)

8. Therefore the angle **AGH** is not unequal to the angle **GHD**; that is, the angle **AGH** is equal to the angle **GHD**.

9. But the angle **AGH** is equal to the angle **EGB**. (*Prop.* 15, *Book* I.)

10. Therefore the angle **EGB** is equal to the angle **GHD**. *Axiom* 1.)

11. Add to each of these the angle **BGH**.

12. Therefore, the angles **EGB, BGH**, are equal to the angles **BGH, GHD**. (*Axiom* 2.)

13. But the angles **EGB, BGH**, are equal to two right angles. (*Proposition* 13, *Book* I.)

14. Therefore, also, the angles **BGH, GHD**, are equal to two right angles.

CONCLUSION.—Wherefore, if a straight line, &c. (*See Enunciation.*) *Which was to be shewn.*

PROPOSITION 30.—THEOREM:

Straight lines, which are parallel to the same straight line, are parallel to each other.

HYPOTHESIS.—Let **AB, CD**, be each of them parallel to **EF**.

SEQUENCE.—**AB** shall be parallel to **CD**.

CONSTRUCTION.—Let the straight line **GHK** be drawn cutting **AB, EF**, and **CD**.

DEMONSTRATION.—1. Because **GHK** cuts the parallel straight lines **AB, EF**, the angle **AGH** is equal to the angle **GHF**. (*Proposition* 29, *Book* I.)

2. Again, because the straight line **GK** cuts the parallel straight lines **EF, CD**, the angle **GHF** is equal to the angle **GKD**. (*Prop.* 29, *Book* I.)

3. And it was shown that the angle **AGK** (*or AGH*) is equal to the angle **GHF**. (*Demonstration* 1.)

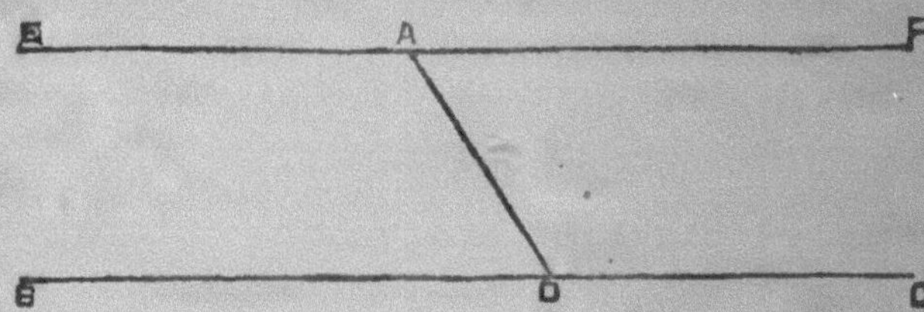

4. Therefore the angle **AGK** is equal to the angle **GKD** (*Axiom* 1), and they are alternate angles.

5. Therefore the straight line **AB** is parallel to the straight line **CD**. (*Prop.* 27, *Book* I.)

CONCLUSION.—Wherefore, straight lines, &c. (*See Enunciation.*) *Which was to be shewn.*

PROPOSITION 31.—PROBLEM.

To draw a straight line through a given point, parallel to a given straight line.

GIVEN.—Let **A** be the given point, and **BC** the given straight line.

SOUGHT.—It is required to draw a straight line through the point **A**, parallel to the straight line, **BC**.

CONSTRUCTION.—1. In **BC** take any point **D**.

2. Join **AD**.

3. At the point **A**, in the straight line **AD**, make the angle **DAE** equal to the angle **ADC**. (*Prop.* 23, *Book* I.)

4. Produce the straight line **EA** to **F**, **EF** shall be parallel to **BC**.

PROOF.—1. Because the straight line **AD** meets the two straight lines **BC, EF**, the alternate angles **EAD, ADC**, are equal to one another.

2. Therefore **EF** is parallel to **BC**. (*Prop.* 27, *Book* I.)

CONCLUSION.—Therefore, the straight line EAF, is drawn through the given point A, parallel to the given straight line, BC. *Which was to be done.*

PROPOSITION 32.—THEOREM.

If a side of any triangle be produced, the exterior angle is equal to the two interior and opposite angles; and the three interior angles of every triangle are equal to two right angles.

HYPOTHESIS.—Let ABC be a triangle, and let one of its sides, BC, be produced to D.

SEQUENCE.—1. The exterior angle, ACD, shall be equal to the two interior and opposite angles, CAB, ABC.

2. And the three interior angles of the triangle, viz., ABC, BCA, CAB, shall together be equal to two right angles.

CONSTRUCTION.—Through the point C, draw CE parallel to AB. (*Prop.* 31, *Book* I.)

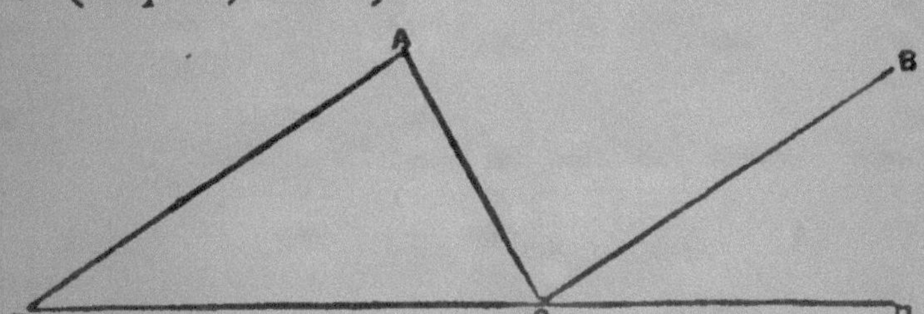

DEMONSTRATION.—1. Because AB is parallel to CE, and AC meets them, the alternate angles BAC, ACE, are equal. (*Prop.* 29, *Book* I.)

2. Again, because AB is parallel to CE, and BD falls on them, the exterior angle, ECD, is equal to the interior and opposite angle, ABC. (*Prop.* 29, *Book* I.)

3. But the angle ACE was shewn to be equal to the angle BAC. (*Demonstration* 1.)

4. Therefore the whole exterior angle ACD (*made up of the angles ACE, ECD*), is equal to the two interior and opposite angles, CAB, ABC. (*Axiom* 2.)

5. To each of these equals, add the angle ACB.

6. The angles ACD, ACB, are equal to the three angles CBA, BAC, ACB. (*Axiom* 2.)

7. But the angles ACD, ACB, are equal to two right angles. (*Prop.* 13, *Book* I.)

8. Therefore, also, the angles CBA, BAC, ACB, are equal to two right angles. (*Axiom* 1.)

D

CONCLUSION.—Wherefore if a side of any triangle, &c. (*See Enunciation.*)   *Which was to be shewn.*

COROLLARY.—I. *All the interior angles of any rectilineal figure, together with four right angles, are equal to twice as many right angles as the figure has sides.*

1. For we can divide any rectilineal figure, ABCDE, into as many triangles as the figure has sides, by drawing straight lines from a point F, within the figure, to each of its angular points.

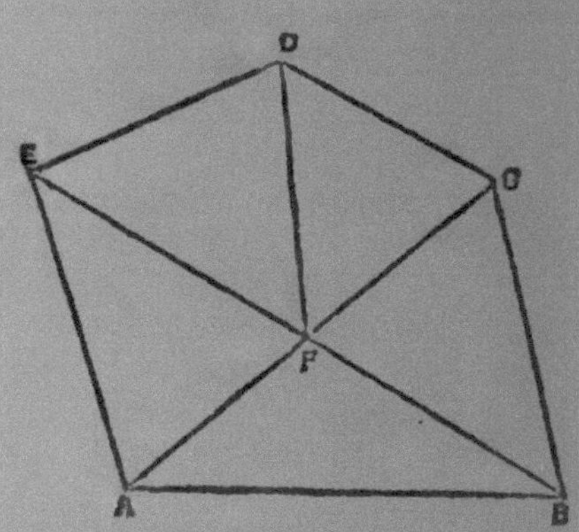

2. Now, by the preceding proposition (*which shews us that the three interior angles of a triangle are equal to two right angles*), we see that all the angles of these triangles must be equal to twice as many right angles as there are triangles.

3. Or, in other terms, that all the angles of these triangles must be equal to twice as many right angles as the figure has sides.

4. But all the angles of these triangles are equal to the angles of the figure, together with the angles at F, the common vertex of the triangles.

5. And the 2*nd Corollary of Prop.* 15, shews us that the angles made by any number of lines meeting together at one point, are equal to four right angles.

6. Therefore the angles made by the meeting of the lines AF, BF, CF, DF, and EF, in the point F, are equal to four right angles.

7. Therefore all the angles of the triangles are equal to the angles of the figure, together with four right angles.

8. And, consequently, all the angles of the figure, together with four right angles, are equal to twice as many right angles as the figure has sides.

COROLLARY.—II. *All the exterior angles of any rectilineal figure, are together equal to four right angles.*

1. The interior angle ABC, with its adjacent exterior angle ABD, are equal to two right angles. (*Prop.* 13, *Book* I.)

2. Therefore all the interior, together with all the exterior angles of the figure, are equal to twice as many right angles as the figure has sides.

3. Therefore, by the foregoing corollary, all the interior, with all the exterior angles of·the figure, are equal to all the interior angles of the figure, together with four right angles.

4. Take away the interior angles of the figure which are common to both, and we find that the exterior angles of the figure remaining on one side, are equal to the four right angles remaining on the other.

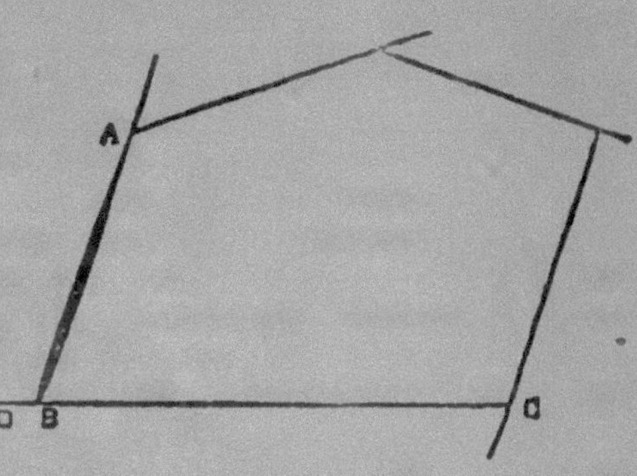

5. Therefore all the exterior angles of any rectilineal figure are equal to four right angles.

PROPOSITION 33.—THEOREM.

The straight lines which join the extremities of two equal and parallel straight lines towards the same parts, are also themselves equal and parallel.

HYPOTHESIS.—Let **AB** and **CD** be equal and parallel straight lines, joined towards the same parts by the straight lines AC, BD.

SEQUENCE.—AC and BD shall also be equal and parallel.

CONSTRUCTION.—Join BC.

DEMONSTRATION.—1. Because AB is parallel to CD, and BC meets them, the alternate angles ABC, BCD, are equal. (*Proposition* 29, *Book* I.)

2. Because AB is equal to CD, and BC common to the two triangles, ABC, DCB, the two sides AB, BC, are equal to the two sides BC, CD, each to each.

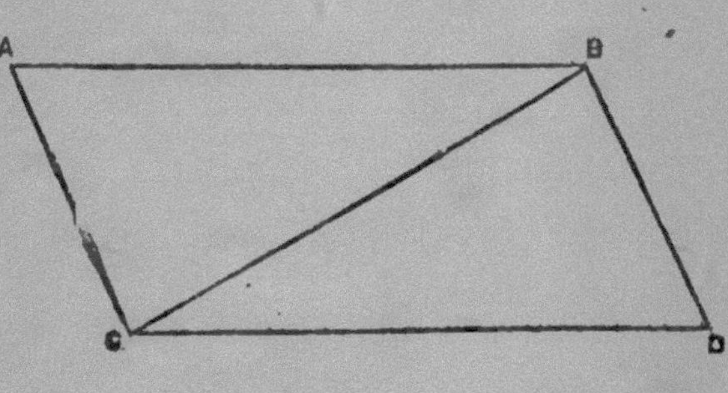

3. And the angle ABC is equal to the angle BCD (*Demonstration* 1.)

4. Therefore the base AC, is equal to the base BD. (*Prop.* 4, *Book* I.)

5. And the triangle ABC, is equal to the triangle BCD. (*Prop.* 4, *Book* I.)

6. And the other angles are equal to the other angles, each to each, to which the equal sides are opposite.

7. Therefore the angle ACB is equal to the angle CBD.

8. And because the straight line BC meets the two straight lines AC, BD, and makes the alternate angles ACB, CBD, equal to one another.

9. Therefore the straight line AC is parallel to BD. (*Prop.* 27, *Book* I.) And AC has been shewn to be equal to BD. (*Demonstration* 4.)

CONCLUSION.—Therefore, straight lines, &c. (*See Enunciation.*) *Which was to be done.*

PROPOSITION 34.—THEOREM.

The opposite sides and angles of parallelograms, are equal to one another, and the diameter bisects them, that is, divides them into two equal parts.

HYPOTHESIS.—Let ABCD be a parallelogram, of which BC is a diameter.

SEQUENCE.—1. The opposite sides and angles of the figure shall be equal to one another.

2. And the diameter BC shall bisect it.

DEMONSTRATION.—1. Because AB is parallel to CD, and BC meets them, the alternate angles, ABC, BCD, are equal to one another. (*Prop.* 29, *Book* I.)

2. Because AC is parallel to BD, and BC meets them, the

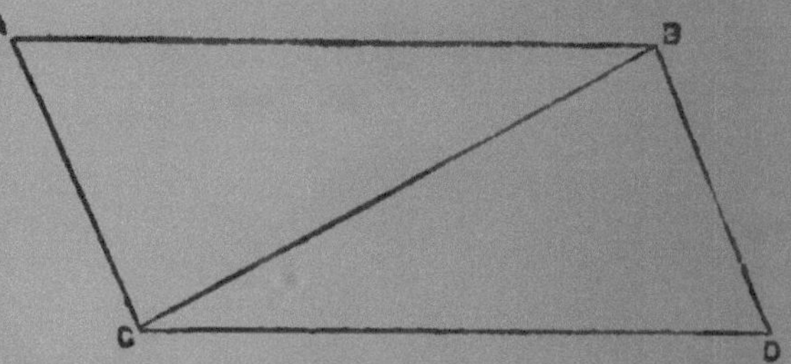

alternate angles ACB, CBD, are equal to one another. (*Prop.* 29, *Book* I.)

3. Wherefore the two triangles ABC, CBD, have two angles, ABC, BCA, in the one equal to two angles, BCD, CBD, in the other each to each.

4. And they have one side, BC, common to both triangles, adjacent to the equal angles in each.

5. Therefore their other sides are equal, each to each; viz., the side AB to the side CD, and the side AC to the side BD. (*Prop.* 26, *Book* I.)

6. And the third angle of the one is equal to the third angle of the other; viz., the angle BAC, equal to the angle BDC. (*Prop.* 26, *Book* I.)

7. And because the angle ABC, is equal to the angle BCD, and the angle CBD to the angle ACB.

8. Therefore the whole angle ABD, is equal to the whole angle ACD. (*Axiom* 2.)

9. And the angle BAC has been shewn to be equal to the angle BDC. (*Demonstration* 6.)

Therefore the opposite sides and angles of parallelograms are equal to one another.

10. Also their diameter bisects them; for AB being equal to CD, and BC common, the two, AB, BC, are equal to the two, BC, CD, each to each.

11. And the angle ABC has been proved equal to the angle BCD. (*Demonstration* 1.)

12. Therefore the triangle ABC is equal to the triangle BCD. (*Prop.* 4, *Book* I.)

And the diameter BC, therefore, divides the parallelogram ABDC into two equal parts.

Conclusion.—Therefore, the opposite sides, &c. (*See Enunciation.*) *Which was to be done.*

PROPOSITION 35.—THEOREM.

Parallelograms upon the same base, and between the same parallels, are equal to one.another.

Hypothesis.—Let the parallelograms ABCD, EBCF, be on the same base BC, and between the same parallels, AF, BC.

Sequence. — The parallelogram ABCD, shall be equal to the parallelogram EBCF.

Case I.—If the sides AD, DF, of the parallelograms ABCD, DBCF, opposite to the base BC, be terminated in the same point D, it is plain that—

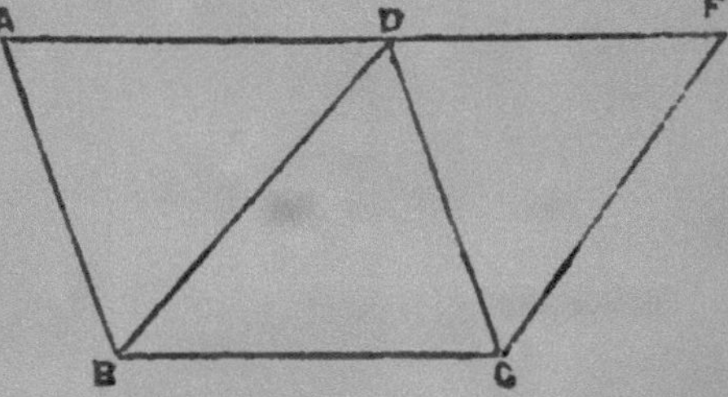

1. Each of the parallelograms is double of the triangle, BDC. (*Prop.* 34, *Book* I.)

2. And that they are therefore equal to one another. (*Axiom* 6.)

CASE II.—But if the sides AD, EF, opposite to the base BC, of the parallelograms ABCD, EBCF, be not terminated in the same point; then—

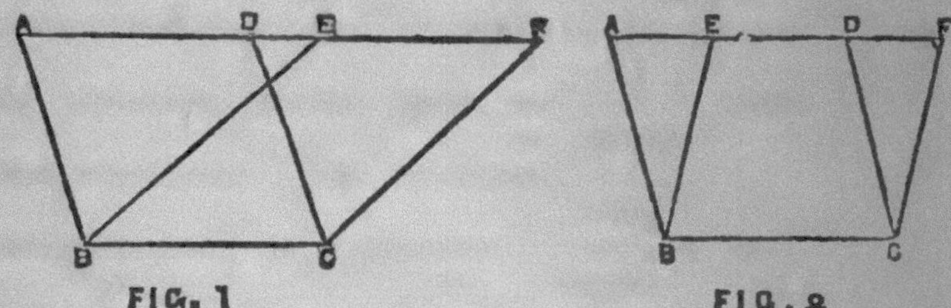

FIG. 1   FIG. 2

DEMONSTRATION.—1. Because ABCD is a parallelogram, AD is equal to BC. (*Prop.* 34, *Book* I.)

2. For the same reason, EF is equal to BC.

3. Wherefore AD is equal to EF (*Axiom* 1), and DE is common.

4. Therefore the whole (*fig. I.*) or remainder (*fig. II.*), AE is equal to the whole (*fig. I.*), or remainder (*fig. II.*), DF, (*Axiom* 2), (*fig. I.*), (*Axiom* 3), (*fig. II.*)

5. And AB is also equal to DC. (*Prop.* 34, *Book* I.)

6. Therefore the two, EA, AB, are equal to the two, FD, DC, each to each.

7. And the exterior angle FDC, is equal to the interior, EAB. (*Prop.* 29, *Book* I.)

8. Therefore the base EB, is equal to the base FC. (*Prop.* 4, *Book* I.)

9. And the triangle EAB equal to the triangle FDC.

10. Take the triangle FDC, from the trapezium ABCF, and from the same (*or from a similar*) trapezium ABCF, take the triangle EAB.

11. The remainders are equal. (*Axiom* 3.) That is to say, the parallelogram ABCD, is equal to the parallelogram EBCF.

CONCLUSION.—Therefore, parallelograms upon the same base, &c. (*See Enunciation.*) *Which was to be shewn.*

The latter part of this demonstration would be rendered more intelligible to the learner's mind, if the operation of taking away the triangles from the trapeziums were actually performed on two similar trapeziums, cut out in paper or card-board. This method is also useful where super-position is required in the demonstration, as in Proposition 4.

PROPOSITION 36.—THEOREM.

Parallelograms upon equal bases, and between the same parallels, are equal to one another.

HYPOTHESIS.—Let ABCD, EFGH, be parallelograms upon equal bases, BC FG, and between the same parallels, AH, BG.

SEQUENCE.—The parallelogram ABCD shall be equal to the parallelogram EFGH.

CONSTRUCTION.—Join BE, CH.

DEMONSTRATION. — 1. Because BC is equal to FG (*Hypothesis*), and FG to EH. (*Proposition 34, Book* I.)

2. BC is therefore equal to EH, (*Axiom* 1,) and they are parallels, (*Hypothesis*,) and joined towards the same parts by the straight lines BE, CH.

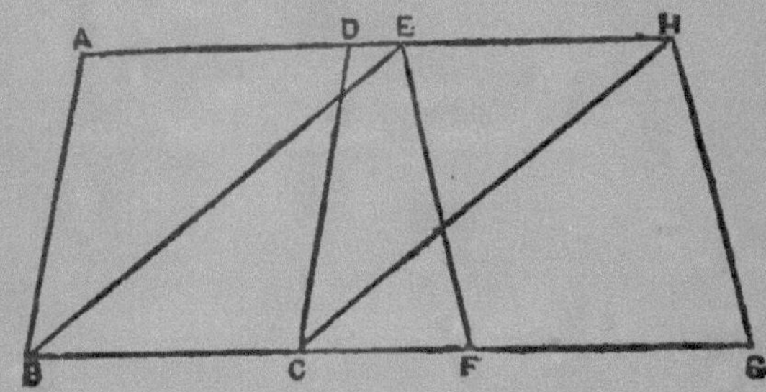

3. But straight lines which join the extremities of equal and parallel straight lines, are themselves also equal and parallel. (*Prop.* 33, *Book* 1.)

4. Therefore the straight lines, BE, CH, are both equal and parallel.

5. And EBCH is a parallelogram. (*Definition* 35, *Note.*)

6. And it is equal to the parallelogram ABCD, because they are on the same base BC, and between the same parallels, BC, AH. (*Prop.* 35, *Book* I.)

7. For the like reason, the parallelogram EFGH is equal to the same EBCH, (*being on the same base EH, and between the same parallels, EH, BG.*)

8. Therefore the parallelogram ABCD is equal to the parallelogram EFGH. (*Axiom* 1.)

CONCLUSION.—Wherefore, parallelograms, &c. (*See Enunciation.*) *Which was to be done.*

PROPOSITION 37.—THEOREM.

Triangles upon the same base, and between the same parallels, are equal to one another.

HYPOTHESIS.—Let the triangles ABC, DBC, be upon the same base, BC, and between the same parallels, AD, BC.

SEQUENCE.—The triangle ABC shall be equal to the triangle DBC.

CONSTRUCTION.—1. Produce AD both ways, to the points E, F.   (*Postulate* 2.)

2. Through B draw BE, parallel to CA, and through C draw CF parallel to BD. (*Prop.* 31, *Book* I.)

3. Therefore each of the figures EBCA, DBCF, is a parallelogram. (*Def.* 35, *Note.*)

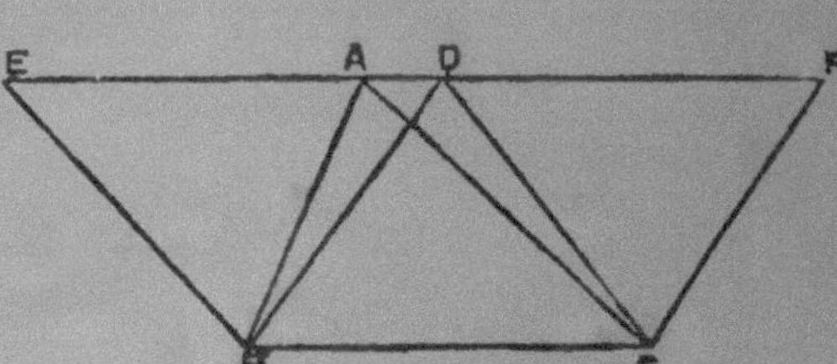

4. And EBCA is equal to DBCF, because they are upon the same base BC, and between the same parallels BC, EF. (*Prop.* 35, *Book* I.)

5. And the triangle ABC is the half of the parallelogram EBCA, because the diameter AB bisects it. (*Prop.* 34, *Book* I.)

6. And the triangle DBC is the half of the parallelogram DBCF, because the diameter DC bisects it.

7. But the halves of equal things are themselves also equal. (*Axiom* 7.)

8. Therefore the triangle ABC is equal to the triangle DBC.

CONCLUSION.— Wherefore, triangles, &c. (*See Enunciation.*) *Which was to be shewn.*

PROPOSITION 38.—THEOREM.

Triangles upon equal bases, and between the same parallels, are equal to one another.

HYPOTHESIS.—Let the triangles ABC, DEF, be upon equal bases BC, EF, and between the same parallels BF, AD.

SEQUENCE.—The triangle ABC shall be equal to the triangle DEF.

CONSTRUCTION.—1. Produce AD both ways to the points G, H. (*Postulate* 2.)

2. Through B draw BG parallel to CA, and through F draw FH parallel to ED. (*Prop.* 31, *Book* I.)

3. Then each of the figures GBCA, DEFH, is a parallelogram. (*Definition* 35, *Note.*)

4. And they are equal to each other, because they are on equal bases, BC, EF, and between the same parallels, BF, GH. (*Prop.* 36, *Book* I.)

5. And the triangle ABC is the half of the parallelogram GBCA, because the diameter AB bisects it. (*Prop* 34, *Book* I.)

6. And the triangle DEF is the half of the parallelogram DEFH, because the diameter DF bisects it. (*Prop.* 34, *Book* I.)

7. But the halves of equal things are equal; therefore the triangle ABC is equal to the triangle DEF. (*Axiom* 7.)

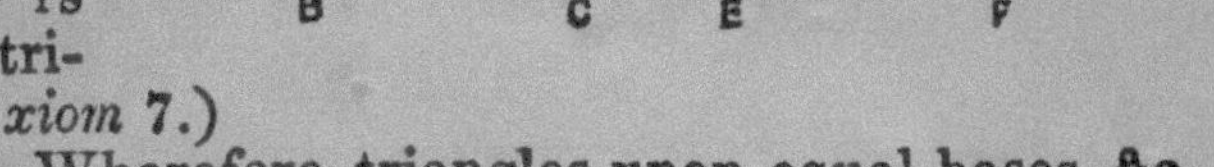

CONCLUSION.—Wherefore triangles upon equal bases, &c. (*See Enunciation.*) *Which was to be shewn.*

PROPOSITION 39.—THEOREM.

Equal triangles upon the same base, and upon the same side of it, are between the same parallels.

HYPOTHESIS.—Let the equal triangles, ABC, DBC, be upon the same base BC, and upon the same side of it.

SEQUENCE.—They shall be between the same parallels; *or, in other words*—Join AD, then AD shall be parallel to BC.

CONSTRUCTION.—1. For if AD is not parallel to BC, through the point A draw AE parallel to BC. (*Prop.* 31, *Book* I.)

2. Join EC.

DEMONSTRATION.—1. The triangle ABC is equal to the triangle EBC, because they are upon the same base BC, and between the same parallels, BC, AE. (*Prop.* 37, *Book* I.)

2. But the triangle ABC is equal to the triangle DBC. (*Hypothesis.*)

3. Therefore the triangle DBC is equal to the triangle EBC (*Axiom* 1), the greater equal to the less, which is impossible.

4. Therefore AE is not parallel to BC.

5. In the same manner it may be demonstrated that no other line but AD is parallel to BC.

6. **AD** is therefore parallel to **BC**.

CONCLUSION.—Wherefore, equal triangles, &c. (*See Enunciation.*) *Which was to be done.*

PROPOSITION 40.—THEOREM.

Equal triangles upon equal bases in the same straight line, and towards the same parts, are between the same parallels.

HYPOTHESIS.—Let the equal triangles **ABC, DEF,** be upon equal bases **BC, EF,** in the same straight line **BF,** and towards the same parts.

SEQUENCE.—The triangles, **ABC, DEF,** shall be between the same parallels; *or, in other words*—Join **AD, AD** shall be parallel to **BF.**

CONSTRUCTION.—1. For if **AD** is not parallel to **BF,** through **A** draw **AG** parallel to **BF.** (*Prop.* 31, *Book* I.)

2. Join **GF.**

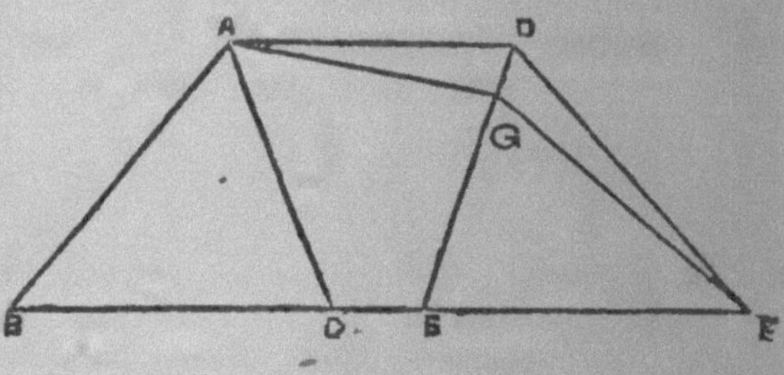

DEMONSTRA-TION.—1. The triangle **ABC** is equal to the triangle **GEF,** because they are upon equal bases, **BC, EF,** and between the same parallels **BF, AG.** (*Prop.* 38, *Book* I.)

2. But the triangle **ABC** is equal to the triangle **DEF.** (*Hypothesis.*)

3. Therefore also the triangle **DEF** is equal to the triangle **GEF** (*Axiom* 1), the greater equal to the less, which is impossible.

4. Therefore **AG** is not parallel to **BF.**

5. And in like manner it can be demonstrated that there is no other parallel to it but **AD.**

6. **AD** is therefore parallel to **BF.**

CONCLUSION.—Wherefore equal triangles, &c. (*See Enunciation.*) *Which was to be shewn.*

PROPOSITION 41.—THEOREM.

If a parallelogram and a triangle be upon the same base, and between the same parallels, the parallelogram shall be doubl *of the triangle.*

HYPOTHESIS.—Let the parallelogram **ABCD,** and the

triangle EBC be upon the same base BC, and between the same parallels, BC, AE.

SEQUENCE.—The parallelogram ABCD shall be double of the triangle EBC.

CONSTRUCTION.—Join AC.

DEMONSTRATION.—1. The triangle ABC is equal to the triangle EBC, because they are upon the same base BC, and between the same parallels BC, AE. (*Prop.* 37, *Book* I.)

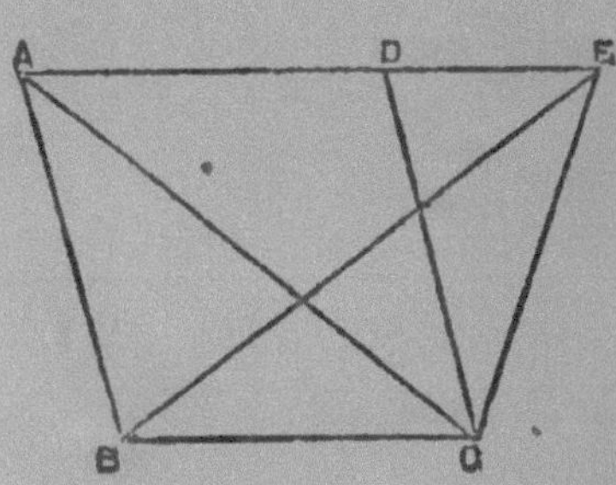

2. But the parallelogram ABCD is double of the triangle ABC, because the diameter AC divides it into two equal parts. (*Proposition* 34, *Book* I.)

3. Wherefore the parallelogram ABCD is also double of the triangle EBC.

CONCLUSION.—Wherefore if a parallelogram, &c. (*See Enunciation.*) *Which was to be done.*

––––––

PROPOSITION 42.—PROBLEM.

To describe a parallelogram that shall be equal to a given triangle, and have one of its angles equal to a given rectilineal angle.

GIVEN.—Let ABC be the given triangle, and D the given rectilineal angle.

SOUGHT.—It is required to describe a parallelogram that shall be equal to the given triangle ABC, and have one of its angles equal to D.

CONSTRUCTION.—1. Bisect BC in E. (*Prop.* 10, *Book* I.)

2. Join AE.

3. At the point E, in the straight line CE, make the angle CEF equal to D. (*Prop.* 23, *Book* I.)

4. Through A draw AFG parallel to EC. (*Prop.* 31, *Book* I.)

5. Through C draw CG parallel to EF. (*Prop.* 31, *Book* I.)

The figure FECG is a parallelogram (*Definition* 35, *Note*), it shall be the parallelogram required.

DEMONSTRATION.—1. Because BE is equal to EC (*Construction* 1), the triangle ABE is equal to the triangle AEC. (*Prop.* 38, *Book* I.)

2. For they are upon equal bases **BE, EC,** and between the same parallels **BC, AG**.

3. Therefore the triangle **ABC** is double of the triangle **AEC**.

4. But the parallelogram **FECG** is likewise double of the triangle **AEC**. (*Prop.* 41, *Book* I.)

5. For they are upon the same base **EC**, and between the same parallels **EC, AG**.

6. Therefore the parallelogram **FECG** is equal to the triangle **ABC**. (*Axiom* 6.)

7. And it has one of its angles **CEF**, equal to the given angle **D**. (*Construction* 3.)

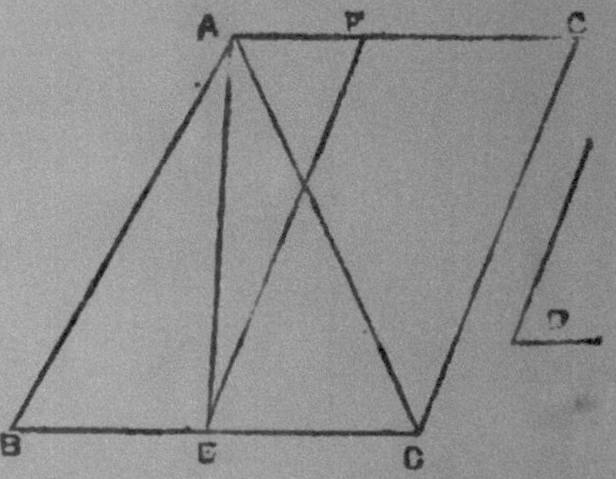

CONCLUSION.—Wherefore a parallelogram **FECG** has been described equal to the given triangle **ABC**, having one of its angles, **CEF**, equal to the given rectilineal angle **D**. *Which was to be done.*

PROPOSITION 43.—THEOREM.

The complements of the parallelograms which are about the diameter of any parallelogram, are equal to one another.

HYPOTHESIS.—Let **ABCD** be a parallelogram, of which **AC** is the diameter (1), and **EH, GF** parallelograms about **AC**, that is, through which **AC** passes (2), and **BK, KD** the other parallelograms, which make up the whole figure **ABCD**, which are therefore called the complements (3).

SEQUENCE.—The complement **BK** shall be equal to the complement **KD**.

DEMONSTRATION.—1. Because **ABCD** is a parallelogram, and **AC** its diameter, the triangle **ABC** is equal to the triangle **ADC**. (*Prop.* 34, *Book* I.)

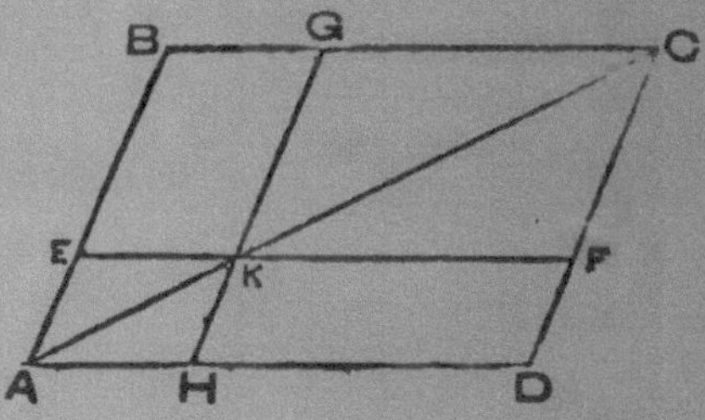

2. Again, because **EKHA** is a parallelogram, the diameter of which is **AK**, the triangle **AEK** is equal to the triangle **AHK**. (*Prop.* 34, *Book* I.)

3. For the same reason the triangle **KGC** is equal to the triangle **KFC**.

4. Therefore because the triangle AEK is equal to the triangle AHK, and the triangle KGC equal to the triangle KFC.

5. The triangles AEK, KGC, are equal to the triangles AHK, KFC. (*Axiom* 2.)

6. But the whole triangle ABC was proved equal to the whole triangle ADC. (*Demonstration* 1.)

7. Therefore the remaining complement BK (*of the whole triangle ABC*), is equal to the remaining complement KD (*of the whole triangle ADC.*)

CONCLUSION.—Wherefore, the complements, &c. (*See Enunciation.*) *Which was to be shewn.*

PROPOSITION 44.—PROBLEM.

To a given straight line to apply a parallelogram, which shall be equal to a given triangle, and have one of its angles equal to a given rectilineal angle.

GIVEN.—Let AB be the given straight line, C the given triangle, and D the given rectilineal angle.

SOUGHT.—It is required to apply to the straight line AB, a parallelogram equal to the triangle C, and having an angle equal to D.

CONSTRUCTION.—(I.) 1. Make the parallelogram BEFG equal to the triangle C, and having the angle EBG equal to D. (*Prop.* 42, *Book* I.)

2. And let the parallelogram BEFG be made so that BE may be in the same straight line with AB.

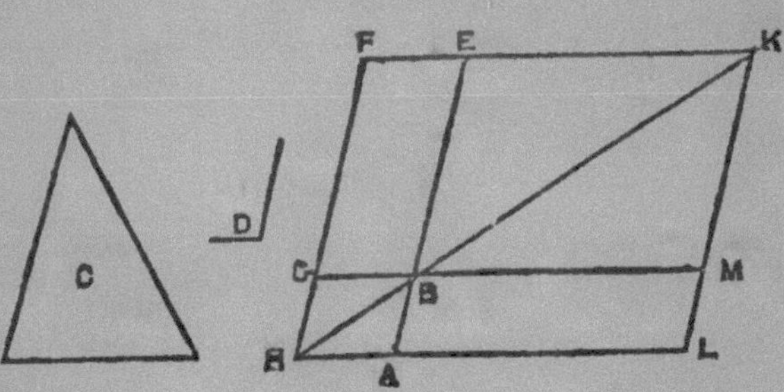

3. Produce FG to H.

4. Through A draw AH parallel to BG or EF. (*Prop.* 31, *Book* I.)

5. Join HB.

PROOF.—(I.) 1. Because the straight line HF falls upon the parallels AH, EF, the angles AHF, HFE are together equal to two right angles. (*Prop.* 29, *Book* I.)

2. Wherefore the angles BHF, HFE, are together less than two right angles.

But straight lines, which with another straight line make the interior angles upon the same side less than two right angles, do meet if produced far enough. (*Axiom* 12.)

3. Therefore HB, FE, shall meet if produced.

CONSTRUCTION.—(II.) 1. Produce HB, FE, towards BE, and let them meet in K.

2. Through K draw KL parallel to EA or FH.

3. Produce HA, GB, to the points L, M.

4. HLKF is a parallelogram, of which the diameter is HK, and AG ME are parallelograms about HK, and LB BF are the complements; LB shall be the parallelogram required.

PROOF.—(II.) 1. Because LB BF are the complements of the whole figure, HLKF, LB is equal to BF. (*Prop.* 43, *Book* I.)

2. But BF is equal to the triangle C. (*Construction* 1.)

3. Therefore LB is also equal to the triangle C. (*Axiom* 1.)

4. And the angle GBE is equal to the angle ABM. (*Prop.* 15, *Book* I.)

5. But the angle GBE is equal to the angle D. (*Construction* 1.)

6. Therefore the angle ABM is also equal to the angle D. (*Axiom* 1.)

CONCLUSION.—Therefore the parallelogram LB is applied to the straight line AB, equal to the triangle C, and having the angle ABM, equal to the angle D. *Which was to be done.*

PROPOSITION 45.—PROBLEM.

To describe a parallelogram equal to a given rectilineal figure, and having an angle equal to a given rectilineal angle.

GIVEN.—Let ABCD be the given rectilineal figure, and E the given rectilineal angle.

SOUGHT.—It is required to describe a parallelogram equal to ABCD, having an angle equal to E.

CONSTRUCTION.—1. Join DB, (*dividing the rectilineal figure ABCD into two triangles, ADB, DBC.*)

2. Describe the parallelogram FKHG, equal to the triangle ADB, and having the angle FKH equal to the angle E. (*Prop.* 42, *Book* I.)

3. To the straight line GH apply the parallelogram

GHML equal to the triangle DBC, having the angle GHM equal to E.   (*Prop.* 44, *Book* I.)

The figure FKML shall be the parallelogram required.

PROOF.—1. Because the angle E is equal to each of the angles FKH, GHM.   (*Construction* 2 *and* 3.)

2. Therefore, the angle FKH is equal to the angle GHM. (*Axiom* 1.)

3. Add to each of these the angle KHG.

4. Therefore, the angles FKH, KHG are equal to the angles KHG, GHM.   (*Axiom* 2.)

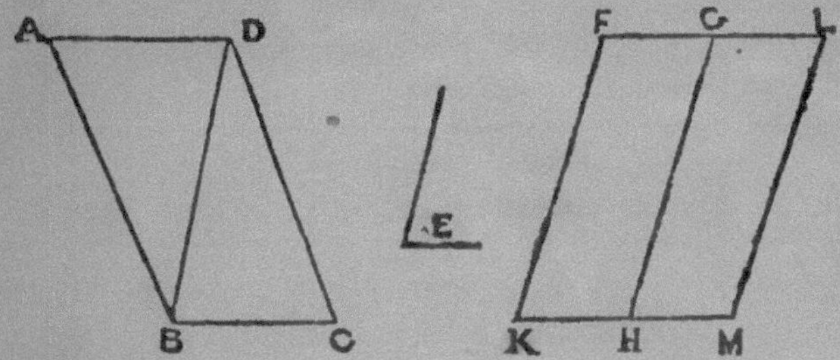

5. But the angles FKH, KHG are equal to two right angles.   (*Prop.* 29, *Book* I.)

6. Therefore, also, the angles KHG, GHM are equal to two right angles.   (*Axiom* 1.)

7. Now because at the point H in the straight line GH, the two straight lines HK, HM, upon opposite sides of it, make the adjacent angles equal to two right angles.

8. Therefore, HK is in the same straight line with HM. (*Prop.* 14, *Book* I.)

9. And because the straight line HG meets the parallels KM, FG, the alternate angles, MHG, HGF are equal. (*Prop.* 29, *Book* I.)

10. Add to each of these the angle HGL.

11. Therefore, the angles MGH, HGL are equal to the angles HGF, HGL.   (*Axiom* 2.)

12. But the angles MHG, HGL are equal to two right angles.   (*Prop.* 29, *Book* I.)

13. Therefore, the angles HGF, HGL are equal to two right angles.

14. And, therefore, FG is in the same straight line with GL (*because at the point* G *in the straight line* HG, *the two straight lines* GF, GL, *upon opposite sides of it, make the adjacent angles equal to two right angles.*)   (*Prop.* 14, *Book* I.)

15. And because KF is parallel to HG, and HG parallel to ML.   (*Construction* 2, 3.)

16. Therefore, KF is parallel to ML. (*Prop.* 30, *Book* I.)

17. And KM, FL are parallels. (*Construction* 2, 3.)

18. Wherefore KFLM is a parallelogram. (*Def.* 35, *Note.*)

19. And because the triangle ABD is equal to the parallelogram HF, and the triangle DBC equal to the parallelogram GM. (*Construction* 2, 3.)

20. Therefore, the whole rectilineal figure ABCD is equal to the whole parallelogram KFLM. (*Axiom* 2.)

CONCLUSION.—Therefore, the parallelogram KFLM has been described equal to the given rectilineal figure ABCD, having the angle FKM equal to the given angle D. *Which was to be done.*

COROLLARY.—*From this it is manifest how to a given straight line to apply a parallelogram which shall have an angle equal to a given rectilineal angle, and shall be equal to a given rectilineal figure, viz., by applying to the given straight line a parallelogram equal to the first triangle ABD, and having an angle equal to the given angle.* (*Prop.* 44, *Book* I.)

PROPOSITION 46.—PROBLEM.

To describe a square upon a given straight line.

GIVEN.—Let AB be the given straight line.

SOUGHT.—It is required to describe a square upon AB.

CONSTRUCTION.—1. From the point A draw AC at right angles to AB. (*Prop* 11, *Book* I.)

2. And make AD equal to AB. (*Prop.* 3, *Book* I.)

3. Through the point D, draw DE parallel to AB. (*Prop.* 31, *Book* I.)

4. Through the point B, draw BE parallel to AD. (*Proposition* 31, *Book* I.) ADEB is a parallelogram. (*Def.* 35, *Note.*)

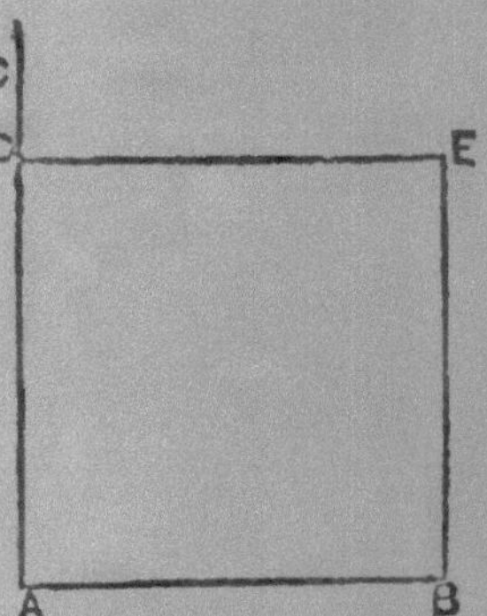

PROOF.—1. Because ADEB is a parallelogram (*Construction* 3, 4), therefore, AB is equal to DE, and AD equal to BE. (*Prop.* 34, *Book* I.)

2. But BA is equal to AD. (*Construction* 2.)

3. Therefore, the four straight lines BA, AD, DE, EB are equal to one another. (*Axiom* 1.)

4. And the parallelogram ADEB is, therefore, equilateral.

5. Because the straight line AD meets the parallels AB,

DE, the angles BAD, ADE, are equal to two right angles (*Prop.* 29, *Book* I.)

6. But the angle BAD is a right angle. (*Construction.*)

7. Therefore, also, the angle ADE is a right angle. (*Axiom* 3.)

8. But the opposite angles of parallelograms are equal. (*Prop.* 34. *Book* I.)

9. Therefore each of the opposite angles ABE, BED is a right angle. (*Axiom* 1.)

10. Therefore, the figure ADEB is rectangular, and it has been shewn to be equilateral. (*Proof* 4.)

CONCLUSION.—Therefore, the figure ADEB is a square (*Definition* 30), and it is described upon the given straight line AB. *Which was to be done.*

COROLLARY.—*Hence every parallelogram that has one right angle, has all its angles right angles.*

PROPOSITION 47.—THEOREM.

In any right angled triangle, the square which is described upon the side subtending the right angle is equal to the squares described upon the sides which contain the right angle.

HYPOTHESIS.—Let ABC be a right angled triangle, having the right angle BAC.

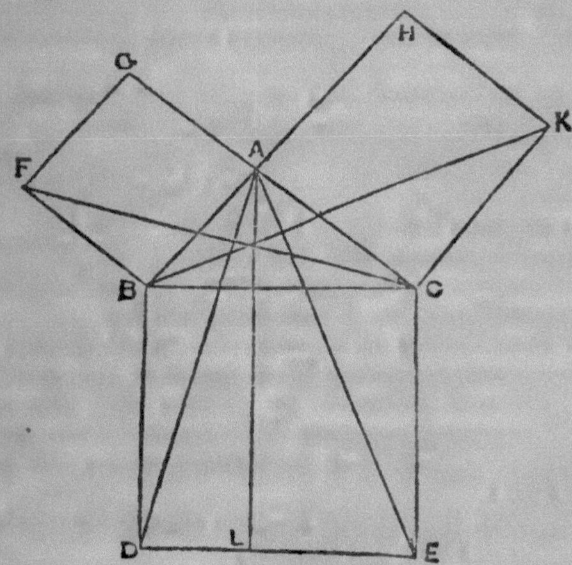

SEQUENCE.—The square described upon the side BC shall be equal to the squares described upon BA, AC.

Construction.—1. On **BC** describe the square **BDEC**. (*Prop.* 46, *Book* I.)

2. On **BA, AC,** describe the squares **ABFG, ACKH.** (*Prop.* 46, *Book* I.)

3. Through **A** draw **AL** parallel to **BD** or **CE**. (*Prop.* 31, *Book* I.)

4. Join **AD, FC.**

Proof.—1. Because the angle **BAC** is a right angle (*Hypothesis*), and that the angle **BAG** is also a right angle. (*Def.* 30.)

2. The two straight lines **AC AG**, upon opposite sides of **AB**, make with it at the point **A** the adjacent angles equal to two right angles.

3. Therefore **CA** is in the same straight line with **AG**. (*Prop.* 14, *Book* I.)

4. For the same reason **AB** and **AH** are in the same straight line.

(*Let the pupil fully shew why AB and AH are in the same straight line.*)

5. And because the angle **DBC** is equal to the angle **FBA** (*Axiom* 11), each of them being a right angle (*Definition* 30), add to each the angle **ABC**.

6. Therefore the whole angle **DBA** is equal to the whole **FBC**. (*Axiom* 2.)

7. And because the two sides **AB, BD**, are equal to the two **FB, BC**, each to each, and the angle **DBA** equal to the angle **FBC**.

8. Therefore the base **AD** is equal to the base **FC**, and the triangle **ABD** to the triangle **FBC**. (*Prop.* 4, *Book* I.)

9. Now the parallelogram **BL** is double of the triangle **ABD**, because they are on the same base **BD**, and between the same parallels **BD, AL**. (*Prop.* 41, *Book* I.)

10. And the square **GB** is double of the triangle **FBC**, because they are on the same base **FB**, and between the same parallels **FB, GC**. *Prop.* 41, *Book* I.)

11. But the doubles of equals are equal to one another, therefore the parallelogram **BL** is equal to the square **GB**.

12. In the same manner, by joining **AE, BK**, it can be shewn that the parallelogram **CL** is equal to the square **HC**.

(*Let the pupil prove that the parallelogram LC is equal to the square HC.*)

13. Therefore the whole square **BDEC** is equal to the two squares **GB, HC**. (*Axiom* 2.)

14. And the square **BDEC** is described on the straight line **BC**, and the squares **GB, HC**, upon **BA, AC**.

15. Therefore the square described upon the side BC, is equal to the squares described upon the sides BA, AC.

CONCLUSION.—Therefore in any right angled triangle, &c. (*See Enunciation.*) *Which was to be shewn.*

PROPOSITION 48.—THEOREM.

If the square described upon one of the sides of a triangle be equal to the squares described upon the other two sides of it, the angle contained by these two sides is a right angle.

HYPOTHESIS.—Let the square described upon BC, one of the sides of the triangle ABC, be equal to the squares described upon the other sides, BA, AC.

SEQUENCE.—The angle BAC shall be a right angle.

CONSTRUCTION.—1. From the point A draw AD at right angles to AC. (*Prop.* 11, *Book* I.)

2. Make AD equal to BA. (*Prop.* 3, *Book* I.)

3. Join DC.

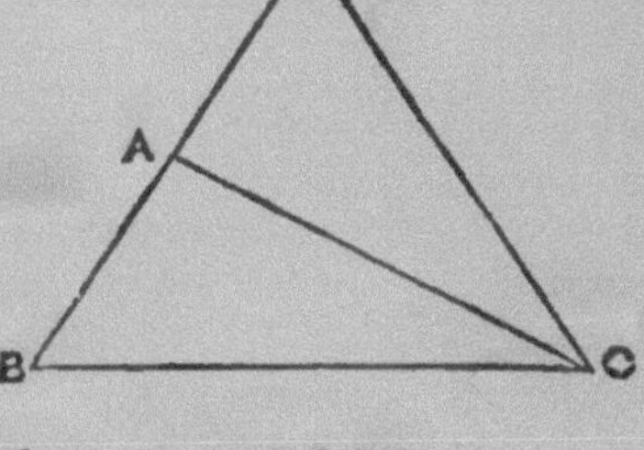

DEMONSTRATION.—1. Because DA is equal to AB, the square of DA is equal to the square of AB.

2. To each of these equals add the square of AC.

3. Therefore the squares of DA AC, are equal to the squares of BA, AC. (*Axiom* 2.)

4. But the square of DC is equal to the square of DA, AC (*Prop.* 47, *Book* I.), because the angle DAC is a right angle. (*Construction* 1.)

5. And the square of BC is equal to the squares of BA, AC. (*Hypothesis.*)

6. Therefore the square of DC is equal to the square of BC. (*Axiom* 1.)

7. And therefore the side DC is equal to the side BC.

8. And because the side DA is equal to AB (*Construction* 2), and AC common to the two triangles DAC, BAC, the two sides DA, AC, are equal to the two BA, AC, each to each.

9. And the base DC has been proved equal to the base BC. (*Proof* 7.)

10. Therefore the angle DAC is equal to the angle BAC. (*Prop.* 8, *Book* I.)

11. But DAC is a right angle. (*Construction* 1.)

12. Therefore, also, BAC is a right angle. (*Axiom* 1.)

CONCLUSION.—Therefore if the square, &c. (*See Enunciation.*) *Which was to be done.*

END OF BOOK I.